things i know

helena close

Little
Island

First published in 2022 by
Little Island Books
7 Kenilworth Park
Dublin 6w
Ireland

A British Library Cataloguing in Publication record for
this book is available from the British Library.

Print ISBN: 978-1-915071033

Little Island has received funding to support this book
from the Arts Council of Ireland

Proofread by Emma Dunne
Cover Design by Anna Morrison
Typeset by Tetragon, London
Printed in Poland by L & C

1 3 5 7 9 10 8 6 4 2

Do mo chara, Rena,
le grá agus buíochas

May

1

'Take the devil out,' says Cian, pushing his big bacon-and-cabbage head right in my face. 'Fuck sake, Saoirse, just give it one good slug – what's wrong with you?'

He grabs the wine bottle from me, some cheap shit from Megan's mother's endless stash, and glugs it back, like water.

'Devil gone,' he says, laughing and scratching his crotch.

Megan and Kate giggle in unison, like they rehearsed it earlier. Dylan and Finn keep talking, their voices low and urgent. Dylan has an arm around Finn, like he's trying to convince him of something. The Clancy twins have finished a full slab of cans between them and are beating the shit out of each other near the waterfall. Cian hands the bottle to Megan and picks up my guitar. My fucking beautiful guitar that I should never have brought. He perches his arse on a flat rock and strums the chords of 'Outnumbered'. His voice is whiney and Americanised, West Clare accent well hidden, and if Dermot Kennedy could hear this version, he'd never sleep again.

It's one week before the stupid Leaving Cert, our last hurrah for the next few weeks, and everything's wrong. Broken. I want to blame them, but it's me. I know that now and I understand why Megan's cold with me. Finn's her twin. There are lots of twins in West Clare and I'd love to know why.

'Saoirse, you're weird as fuck tonight,' Cian says, giving up on the singing and reverting to his real talents, drinking and being a dick. 'Weirder than usual, like.'

He laughs, looking around for joke validation. He gets none. 'Why didn't your pal come, the mad wan from Limerick? She's a great laugh, her. Thought she was all on for a party?'

He scratches his arse this time – just for a change. I shrug and take a can from the pile on the grass near me. To have something to hold. To play with. I watch Finn and Dylan and am relieved when I see them laughing. At least *they* won't end up beating the crap out of each other too. Then Finn goes all Heathcliff, big moody head on him. He even has the dark curls and he fixes me with his eyes, spearing me, X-raying me. Dylan's all golden lad beside him, shimmery shine off him, even from here. The moon has risen over the rapids and the sun's setting over the forest, and that's one thing I love about the west coast – the way moon and sun drag out the day. There's this space between, a no-time space that I'd like to live in, and I really want Finn to stop staring at me. I pop the can and the cheap beer is warm and smells of vomit. Cian has taken to flicking bottle caps at Megan and Kate. Some fucking party.

Why didn't Jade come, after I begged her to? I pleaded with her, told her how awkward it would be with Finn, how Megan was being weird with me, how I just needed her to come here to this god-forsaken hole for one last time before I could escape back to Limerick and college. Bitch. She probably met someone, and when Jade has a new interest it's like her brain is a wiped hard drive. I miss her. She was great when we moved here first, two years ago, and I didn't know anyone and I was sad and Mam was gone and ... and not much has changed. Mam is still dead, Dad's still living a borrowed life, and maybe so am I. This one doesn't fit. It's tight and loose at the same time and I can't pull it off no matter what I do. Fuck. Cian is right. I'm weird and it's funny that he's the one that picks up on it. Big Clare head on him, no brain, itchy balls, and he can smell an imposter from three fields away.

'Play a few tunes, Saoirse,' he says now, like he knows I'm thinking about him. Megan laughs and turns her back to us. I've seen a lot of Megan's back recently, at school, in town, at the beach. Her back has become more familiar than her face. Cian finishes the wine in one slug and throws the bottle against the rocks under the waterfall. The crash of glass sends crows and conversations skittering.

'What's wrong with ye at all? We're supposed to be partying, like – I'd more fun at my grandmother's funeral. I'm getting locked, so fuck ye,' Cian says, and he unscrews a naggin. He downs it without flinching – only possible when you've an iron stomach and no brain. He grabs my guitar and starts to play, beating the strings into tuneless submission, and a black knob of anger rises in my chest, squeezing air from my lungs. I could feel it when he smashed the bottle, the tiny hello of it in the pit of my stomach, and if I open my mouth now it'll come out like a fist and hammer the fuck out of him.

It's Finn who cops it. Feels it. And he's over and talking to Cian and taking the guitar away from him and my eyes are blurry with tears and rage and something else. Loneliness. Weirdness. I don't know what to call it.

'He's out of it,' Finn says, crouching in front of me. 'Are you OK?'

Cian has the guitar again and Finn tries to grab it from him, but Cian's enjoying this new sport. I get up, but my legs are shaking and I know that the black fist in my chest is bursting to get out.

Cian holds the guitar up in the air. 'Go on, Finn, jump for it, hahaha, watch Finn, lads, wimp is all he is,' he says. He falls backwards, the guitar slipping out of his hands and thumping down towards the river. One of the Clancy twins grabs it before it hits the water. Megan's recording the pantomime for TikTok or Insta because if it's not on her feed then it didn't happen.

'Come on, we'll go into town and get something to eat,' says Dylan, as he grabs my guitar and slips it into its soft case. Finn stacks all the cans and bottles into a neat pile and I can see his eyes searching for the nearest bin. I like that about him.

'We can head out to the beach after the grub – and fuck it, some of us need soakage,' says Dylan. 'You're coming to the beach, aren't you, Saoirse? There's a gang out there already – Iron Blake, Lanky, they've a fire going and all.'

'I don't know,' I say. 'I've work in the morning,'

'I forgot,' says Dylan. 'The new job. Come for a while anyway. Jaysus, we need a decent singer or we'll have Cian howling for the night.'

The last thing I feel like doing is singing. For them.

We're walking the brow of the hill beyond the roaring waterfall and the sky blackens. Starlings swoop in a moving murmuration over and back across the pink and navy sky. I'm laughing and pointing but only Finn looks up too. I never saw a murmuration until I moved here and I think now that this is TikTok-worthy, Insta-perfect, and the others don't even notice. They call starlings *shitlings*. The birds weave intricate paths and I'm shivering and scared and happy all at once.

We walk into town in a long straggle, Dylan and I leading the way, Cian walking in the middle of the road, forcing motorists to swerve and honk at him. He loves that and gives them the finger and shouts long, loud strings of swears after them. He's very articulate when it comes to swearing. This town, Cloughmore, has a whole lexicon of swears that I had to master. If you don't swear, you're weird. I think that's why they all love Jade. She'd come on visits and teach them new swear words and a lot more besides.

We turn down Main Street and head towards Manny's. The street's deserted, although I can hear the sound of a squeeze box coming from one of the pubs and the loud buzz of alcohol-infused chat.

'What are you getting, Saoirse? Let me guess – the veggie option,' says Dylan, leaning in to me as we go in the door. I laugh. The veggie option in Manny's is a garlic chip.

'The usual, love?' Manny asks. Manny was the first person I spoke to when I moved here. It was September, the beginning of fifth year. I had no friends. Manny filled the gap with chips and smiles.

'Extra garlic sauce,' I say and root in my bag for coins. 'How are things?'

'Good, Saoirse. What will you have, young man?'

'Same as her,' says Dylan. 'I can't eat meat in front of her. She guilts me out.'

'She's bad for business, and now she's crossed over to the other side – that fancy place over the road – the competition,' says Manny. He laughs and turns back to his bubbling chip pans.

Cian and the others crowd into the tiny space and it's like they use up all the air and the black fist in my chest squeezes my lungs. *Not here, please not here, in front of them.* I push my way out, past Cian with his sweaty breath and Megan and her sickening perfume and the clingy smell of chips. I crouch down by the window and suck in cold air and try to steady my breathing. I want to go home, but I know staying is the right thing to do. Staying will make the broken seem fixed.

The street is night-quiet, except for the chatter from Manny's and the whish of faraway traffic. Dylan comes out and moves my guitar to sit beside me. He doesn't say anything, doesn't need to pack the silence or look at his

14

phone or flick bottle caps or make jokes. The streetlight throws yellowed, dirty colour on his face but he's still golden. Maybe it's the blond hair and I want to ask him if he bleaches it or highlights it and sure his mother is a hairdresser, the only one in town bar Hair Today and they only do blue rinses and bobs. How do I even know these things? Am I all small-town now too, and fuck it, I can't wait to get out of here.

I see movement at the top of the road and small-town me scans the street. I see a shape, just standing there, and I think it's Finn and I think he's watching us, eyes fixed on mine. I'm about to wave but he disappears around the corner, back towards Lord's Cove, like a shadowy ghost lad. Maybe I imagined him and he's inside getting chips and the double burger he loves, the meatier the better. It wouldn't be the first time I imagined things, people, conversations that never happened.

I stand up, legs cramping and look through the steamed-up window. Megan and Kate are Insta-ing or TikTokking or Snapchatting and Cian's shovelling chips into his mouth. The Clancy twins are leaning against the far wall, chatting like normal people. No sign of Finn. I search the street again but it's deserted. I'm about to ask Dylan if he saw Finn, when the others arrive.

'Here,' says Cian, throwing a parcel of food at Dylan. Cian leans against the window, pawing through a box of chicken, fingers shiny with grease. Dylan unwraps our chips and the waft of garlic makes my stomach growl. Megan and Kate are in a whisper-coven by the doorway. I miss Jade.

15

The air is full of munching sounds, mostly Cian sucking and gnawing at a drumstick like some neanderthal who hasn't seen food in a year. I eat a few chips but the smell of meat sickens me, makes me dizzy and mad. I'm close to punching Cian, just a quick hard fist right between his eyes, because he is everything that's broken, him with his greasy sucking lips and big brazen dumb head and thick accent and homophobic, racist, tiny brain.

'Where's Finn?' he says now, chicken flesh flying out of his mouth.

'Dunno,' says Dylan. 'He was here a while ago. Hey, Meg, where's Finn?'

'No idea,' she says without turning around. 'Probably headed to the beach.'

'Did he say anything to you, Saoirse?'

Cian's eyes narrow as he looks at me. I'm fixated on the bits of meat stuck between his teeth. I shake my head.

'Weird he said nothing. Just fucked off, like,' he says.

He's still looking at me. Bastard.

'I'm going home,' I say and bin my half-eaten chips. I pick up my guitar case and head up the street.

'Wait up,' says Dylan. 'Come to the beach for a few cans.'

'You're some *craic*, Saoirse,' says Cian, but he and the others follow us.

'He's a gowl,' says Dylan. 'He just can't help himself.'

'Stop stealing my words.'

'You own the word "gowl", do you?' Dylan says, laughing.

'Yep. My claim to fame. I brought the word to Cloughmore.'

'Weird night, isn't it, Saoirse? I don't know if we're at the end of something, or at the beginning.'

I know exactly what Dylan means. It's the in-between space, the liminal place where I've been skulking for the last two years.

'I have a question,' I say. I can hear the others screeching and laughing, and when I turn I see them behind us, poking at something in a doorway.

'Ask me anything,' says Dylan.

'Highlights. You get your mother to do highlights for you, don't you?'

He cracks up, spitting chips he's laughing so much. There's a low moaning sound and we turn back towards the lads. Cian's pulling down his fly and aiming at a humped pile in the doorway. My black fist punches up my mouth and comes out in a roar as I realise what he's doing. He's pissing on Timber Hanley, the local town drunk. The fucking bastard is pissing on a passed-out man on the ground. I launch myself at Cian, big, hulky Cian, and he bats me off like a fly. I can't hear the others, their voices are jumbled together, but I can see the flash of Megan's phone or maybe it's Kate's, and hot steam rises from poor Timber on his makeshift doorway bed and I throw myself on Cian's back this time, clinging hard and the piss is a huge arc falling on Timber's face and hair and clothes. I can't get a proper hold of Cian and he's belly-laughing at my attempts and then his ear is there, right by my mouth, soft and hurtable, and I bite down, hard as I can. It feels good. I bite for the guitar, the dumb head on him, the itchy balls and arse, but most of all I bite for Timber.

17

Dylan has me in an armlock and Cian's roaring, clutching his ear and screaming at me, spit flying out of his mouth, and I want to tell him that his pants are down around his ankles and we can all see his little dangly penis and his spotty boxers. Dylan's saying something but it sounds far away and under water. Cian's wiping his ear and his hand's covered in something shiny and black. He's staring at it, pants still down, the absolute gowl. I feel sated, tired, spent. I push Dylan's arms away and kneel beside Timber, who's oblivious still. The smell of strong piss wafts around me. I take off my hoodie and wipe his face with it. I stand up and see the Clancy twins holding my guitar case and I don't know how they got it or why they seem to have the job of rescuing it all night. They step back from me as I grab it from them, and I walk away as Dylan debates following me or seeing what the damage is to Cian's stupid ear. I manage to elbow Megan in the back as I pass her, stupid bitch, and head towards home, but it's a run, not a walk, and the guitar slaps off my back as I turn down towards our house. My phone beeps. A message from Jade.

> Where are u?
> At beach with Nicky and the others.
> Beers cooling. Hurry tf up.

Who the fuck is Nicky? I stare at the screen as a symphony of notifications pops up. I click on one. There it is. A TikTok of me screaming and biting Cian's ear. Snapchat too. And Insta stories. The Cloughmore Vampire. The notifications keep pinging and my eyes sting and of course there's no context, no arc of piss on Timber Hanley's face. I throw the phone hard at the low stone wall in front of our cottage. It shatters and spills its insides on the road. My breathing is raggy and I pick up the mangled phone and allow myself to cry.

2

I can see the school from here, high on the hill, same as the graveyard, and that's fitting. I can see the long, low building, no trees, no flowers, nothing to suggest any kind of joy, just a grey series of rectangles, like an open prison. The coffee machine hisses, and I spill precious liquid as I fumble with the espresso cup. Fuck. This barista shit is hard, even after the YouTube tutorials. All ninety-seven of them.

Joey, the owner, is a young old hippie so the music is ancient, Neil Young's *Harvest*, vinyl of course, which makes poor Neil's voice shake when customers walk across the wooden floor. The machine hisses again and I refill the espressos. I place them on a tray and take them to the customers at the window table.

'There you go. Two espressos,' I say, placing the cups down in front of a middle-aged couple.

'Jaysus, they're fierce small. I told you, Marion, we should have gotten the pot of tea,' says the man, a local from out by us. 'Aren't you whathisname's daughter, am ... the chicken man. Aren't you the chicken man's daughter?'

'I am. Will that be all?'

''Tis nice to see this place open again. 'Twas Burke's hardware, sure I bought all my stuff here. I was only saying it to you last night, Marion, wasn't I ...' His voice trails off as I cross the floor, almost in a run, making Neil Young screech and jump a verse. *Last night.* I can't think of last night and I'm glad I smashed my stupid phone. If I can't see it, it didn't happen and certainly not the TikTok version. I busy myself behind the counter, cleaning and arranging the displays of super salads, feta cheese rolls and halloumi wraps. The Bad Seed is open almost two weeks and I can still get the smell of paint, unleaded of course, and the café has that echoey newness despite the driftwood theme and fishing nets. This is the first vegetarian café in Cloughmore and, judging by the reaction of the locals, it may be the last. I had twelve requests last weekend for bacon and cabbage and three for stew with a bit of bread and butter. Timber Hanley is the only person so far that could be considered a regular. He's getting very fond of his Americano and halloumi wrap. And there it is again. Timber Hanley. Last fucking night.

Joey comes out to clean the tables in his chef's attire and chats to customers as he works. He's Canadian and I suppose that excuses the madness of setting up a veggie café in a market town full of beef and sheep farmers. He's convinced the surfers and tourists from the seaside village two miles away will flock here when word gets out. I'm not

21

so sure but am glad of a summer job – a very rare thing in this part of the world. What will be rarer, though, is if Joey and his pregnant wife manage to make the rent on this place. The job application required the applicant to be vegetarian so that ruled out, well, almost everyone in town except me.

It's the post-lunch lull as Joey says and I haven't the heart to say that the lull is kind of an all-day one and I clean the coffee machine and remind myself not to look out the window at that school. Two more weeks in that hell-hole and I'll never have to go in there again. Ever. A gaggle of girls comes through the door, loud happy voices bouncing off the ceiling full of nets. It's like I fucking summoned them by thinking about that school. I polish the worktop, head bent like I'm performing micro-surgery, but it's no use. My body has other plans and I know how these plans work – the bubbling gurgle in my stomach, the sweaty hands, the stupid racing heart. I feel dizzy and sick, and bend down to try to deep breathe it away, but I can't get enough air into my lungs and my stomach is a volcano now, making whistling whale sounds. Fucking hell. Last night.

'Am ... can we have three cappuccinos, please?'

At least it's Kate and not Megan. The whale noises in my belly whisper and nudge each other, like they're waiting for the exact right moment to be, well, spectacular. I love Neil Young and his whiney voice at this moment.

'Sure,' I say, peering intently at the worktop. 'I'll drop them down.'

'He had to have two stitches, you know.'

'Maybe he shouldn't have pissed on a sleeping man, Kate.' I smile and crank up the coffee machine. She's still standing there. 'Anything else? Or would you like to make a TikTok? A Snapchat?'

'It was just a laugh, that's all.'

'Yeah. Sure. Hilarious.' I watch as the coffee drips into cups, slow and lazy. I can feel her eyes on me. The whale noises are loud now. Jesus, she must be able to hear them. My hands shake as I bang coffee grinds into the bin. Why did they even come in here? Bitches. I can hear the others chatting, Megan laughing at something. My stomach is having a full-blown conversation with itself, little whale sounds cooing and gurgling and having the chats. It's like they've missed each other, haven't spoken since my last meltdown a few weeks ago. I put the coffees on a tray and push it towards her. Froth tips over the cups and drips down to the saucer. Good. She takes the tray and walks towards her friends.

I need the toilet, but I'll have to pass them. The volcano bubbles once again and the air around me feels dry and hot. I walk towards them, concentrating on the bathroom door, but it's like my eyes aren't listening to my brain. I'm looking straight at her, at Megan, and she stares right through me like I am glass. Invisible. Non-existent. Cancelled. In that moment a punch, a slap, a kick, would have felt better. Kinder.

*　　*　　*

Go away, Mam, you're no help and you're in my head. You're not in my head? Then how do I stop it? Remember when I was small and we'd read Chicken Licken and the sky was falling in and now it is and I can't stop so what do I do? Not talking today, Mam? I didn't mean to bite him. That's a lie. I'm glad I did and it's easy for you when you're not even here any more. I've tried all our old tricks. Even the hospital one doesn't work any more. Our groups. We were so good at it. A parliament of owls. A pandemonium of parrots. A fever of stingrays. A scurry of squirrels …

'Saoirse? Are you feeling OK?' Joey's outside the door, tapping lightly.

I'm sitting on the floor of the bathroom and I can't remember how I got here. I can feel her around me, Mam, and almost smell her classroom-chalk scent. In my head. Not real. I jump up and splash water on my face. I look like shit but that's normal. I open the door.

'I'm grand. I just needed a bathroom break.' I smile at him and brace myself as I cross the floor towards the counter. They're gone. The table's already cleared. Joey's packing. The sea is calling him earlier every day. I begin wrapping the salads and leftover sandwiches.

'Saoirse, are you all right?'

I give him my best smile. My happy face. 'Perfect. I'll cash and lock up.'

'Those girls.'

'Women.'

'Those … young women, they upset you, didn't they?'

'No. They're just … you know.' I have a sudden flashback of Cian's ear and my mouth and black blood. Not very

24

vegetarian and I don't think Joey'd understand. 'It's the study, you know, the Leaving Cert is just pressure and ...'

'Look, you don't need to work if that's adding to your stress – I can get somebody else in ...'

'No. The job helps, and it's only weekends until the exams are done,' I say, smiling. *Fuck. I need this job.* 'You'd want to make tracks before the surf's gone.'

Surf doesn't go anywhere. It doesn't just up and go, but I want to be alone here. The café door opens and I don't recognise her first: she's taller, ganglier and embroidered in tattoos, including a spider one on her neck, like he's crawling up to her chin.

'Jade!' My voice is almost a scream.

'Saoirse. Bitch. Where were you last night? I was, like, there all night waiting for you and I texted and rang a million times and Nicky thinks I invented you and what about Cian? I cracked up laughing and ...'

I'm shushing her as Joey lugs a surfboard from the storage room and carries it through the café.

'Joey, this is my friend from Limerick. This is Jade.'

'Hi, Jade. Help yourself to some food – cake – coffee. See you, Saoirse.'

I hold the door open as he manoeuvres the surfboard through. Jade is already rummaging in the fridge, like it's home.

'Come on, show me your coffee skills. I've had a very fucking long night.'

She grabs a sandwich and flops down on the couch near the window seat and takes off her leather bomber jacket.

She's wearing a rust-red T-shirt with *Fuck the Patriarchy* emblazoned across the front. Her arms are tattoo intricacies that would take you a week to decipher and read. Her hair is short and blue and her eyes are feathered in eyeliner. I love those eyes, darty and seeing and clever. Jade. I know her since pre-school and this is how I always imagined she would be as an adult. Mad wild energy and a smell of danger off her that's both intoxicating and terrifying. She's horsing into her sandwich, wiping her mouth with her hand. I bring over her coffee and sit opposite her, inhaling her energy.

'Not having any?' Her mouth is full as she talks. 'Sandwich is all right, like, but it could do with a lump of chicken, you know, something meaty.'

'My stomach's acting up again ...'

'Not surprised. Human-ear dinners can do that.' She laughs at her joke and takes a sip of the steaming coffee. 'Not bad, Saoirse, not bad. I never pegged you for a barista. Brain surgeon maybe – are you still obsessed with how the brain works or have you moved on ... to how ears taste?'

Another guffaw from her and I smile in spite of myself.

'So, like, I went out to Lord's Cove with Nicky because we left Limerick late and there was a huge crowd there and no Saoirse and Cunty Cian arrived clutching his ear and showing it to everyone. Fuck it, Saoirse, it was hilarious. Still bleeding. A bit hanging off and all and his mammy had to pick him up.'

She stops to breathe and that's the thing about Jade: she's like a thought vomit and I always get sucked into her mad helter-skelter. They diagnosed her with ADHD years ago but she just thinks at high speed.

'So Dylan filled me in on what happened – I'd do him just for the hair – and your ex was there, the lovely Finn, and guess where I stayed last night? Me, from the tiny house in Thomondgate – you're lucky you don't have four giant brothers and one bathroom – drives me mad. Guess? Guess?'

I'm trying to digest all the information she just spewed. 'No idea. A tent?'

She laughs. 'Eejit. Me in a tent – I'd rather sleep standing up. The Cascades Hotel – the posh one near the river. It wasn't a room, it was a suite. Me prancing around in my white fluffy robe and slippers. I was like the queen of Cloughmore. I robbed them by the way – the robe, slippers and all the toiletries. Nicky's flush.'

'How?' I don't know any people my age who are flush. The opposite is true.

A shrug from her and a flick of blue hair from her forehead. 'Dunno. IT shit, start-ups or something. And he does all the ents events for the colleges. I'll get him to book you – you're still coming to college in Limerick, aren't you? You're not sneaking off to Trinity – full of posers and posh wans. UL won't know what hit it, though I've done fuck all work – failed my mocks and all.' She takes another sip of her coffee and examines my face.

'How are you?' She reaches out a hand and grips mine and I want to fall into her, just glue myself to her and let her absorb me, take me into that Speedy Gonzales head and block everything out.

'I'm OK,' I say, picking at my fingernails. They're in an awful state.

'Yeah. Sure. Is it the Leaving Cert? Is the Alzheimer's back?'

Jade has a way of phrasing things that's blunt and true and disturbing. When my mother died, I kind of lost my memory. Took a little jaunt out of myself and my city and ended up in Kilrush, sixty miles away, wandering around like an eejit. I don't remember much about it but Jade never forgets the minute details.

'I'm ruling out the exams,' she says, 'because you could have done them last year with a perfect score. What's going on?'

I shake my head. 'I don't know.'

'Are you still seeing that gowl, the therapist fella? Sure he'll be no help with his candles and his salt lamp. Maybe you need medication? They put me on some and I swear I haven't looked back. I'm much calmer, easier with myself. Brain silencers – little blue pills – that's what you need.' She's saying this with a straight face. She believes it. 'Look, Saoirse. I talked to Finn a bit last night and –'

'You shouldn't have. I don't like people having conversations about me.'

'Fuck. Don't look online so. And by the way, I rang, messaged, all night and no answer?'

'I smashed my phone.'

'You dropped it? I hate when that happens.'

'No. I smashed it full force off a wall.'

She looks at me, round dark eyes trying to find answers. 'Mightn't be such a bad idea with all the shit they're posting.

Vicious little fuckers when they want to be. I'd have done the same as you. I'd have bit his dick off and spat it into a river. Gowl.'

'Where and who is Nicky?' I ask this so that I can move the conversation away from me. 'Male or female?'

'Male. He is such a fucking ride, I swear, Saoirse.'

'So you're not gay any more?'

'Bi. I was always bi. All of us are but we don't know it. That's why there's so much internalised homophobia in the world. We can't accept our bi-ness. Is that a word? Anyway, it is now. I like it.'

So much information with Jade. It's like watching a movie on fast forward.

'How are the lads? Your dad and his chickens? I love your little farm but I'd sooner live in a slum in Mumbai – I need life, cities and noise. That's me.'

'Eva's the same. All picture, no brain. Aran's like Dad's silent shadow. Dad's chicken army has grown. He's very proud of his eggs. How are your lot?'

She's just about to launch into a rant when there's a rap on the window. I look up. There's a man outside, hair cut tight to hide a receding hairline, slitty sloe eyes, shiny sallow face. Handsome for an old guy. He's wearing a pink T-shirt with *This is what a feminist looks like* emblazoned across the front. What's with all the slogans? Is that a new Limerick thing? Already I'm composing Cloughmore ones in my head. *Fuck the ploughing championships. Slurry rocks. This is what a dairy farmer looks like.*

'That's him, that's Nicky,' says Jade and jumps up.

'So you're literally fucking the patriarchy,' I say, as she laughs and opens the locked door. Nicky strolls in, nods at me, pulls Jade close, hands on her arse and kisses her full on, tongues and all. The air changes in the room – I can feel it but can't articulate it. He's older, years older than us and what the fuck is he doing with a schoolgirl?

3

'Hi, princess,' he says, pulling away from Jade and examining her like she's his favourite piece of tech. His accent is Limerick, but with the rough edges badly disguised.

Princess. Feminist my hole. The way he says it gives me raggy breathing, sweaty hands. All the trimmings. I'm waiting for the whale noises to start up again. I'm trying to catch Jade's eye, read where she's going with this, but she's all girly and giggly and adoring, touching his face and his baldy head. I don't realise I've fainted until I'm on the floor and this Nicky guy lifts me up and sits me down in the cosy nook and pushes a soft cushion behind my back. It feels hot in here, central heating hot, and I can't hear the traffic outside or the big retro fridge humming or the wall clock ticking. It's like there's a river in my head ready to burst its banks. My chest is tight as a fist. I gulp dry air. Jade walks behind the counter and comes back with a glass of water. She hands it to me and I drink it, tasting the metal hardness.

'Sorry, I'm sorry, I ... I don't feel well today,' I say, addressing a piece of driftwood right over their heads.

Jade laughs. 'Finish the water, Saoirse. Sure I know what you're like, a stressbag. Nicky, this is my best friend in the whole world and you better like her or I'm done with you.'

'Hi, Saoirse – don't worry, I always have that effect on women – they go weak for me,' he says, little rat eyes assessing me.

'Cluckmore is a weird little town, isn't it?' He smiles and his eyes have more wrinkles than Mick Jagger.

Cluckmore. Good incorrect pronunciation but a mad part of me feels defensive and protective of a town I hate.

'I didn't say it right, did I?' He smiles again, arm around Jade's narrow shoulders.

'It's Clough – like clock – clough is a stone, so it means big stone.'

He laughs. 'Big stone last night anyway. They're mad for rock down here. Hey, babe, I've another meeting, pick you up later?'

Babe. For fuck sake. Babe.

Jade turns her face up to his and they start the tongue wrestling again and my angry chest-fist is bubbling and seething and I want to punch his big shiny head. I clear away the cups and glasses, legs still shaky, and get the keys and my bag. They're still at the tongue combat.

'I've to close up,' I say.

Jade pulls away from Shiny Head. 'I'll go out to yours, Saoirse, until Nicky's done. I want to see the lads anyway.'

'I'll pick you up there – send me the coordinates,' says Nicky.

Gowl. You would need more than Google Maps to find bog roads around Cloughmore. I shake the door to hurry them on.

We're out in the evening street, sun dappling the other side of the road. Jade and Nicky are saying their goodbyes and you'd swear he was going off to war. Timber Hanley staggers towards us, can of Bavaria in hand. He's waving it in the air. He's also wearing a leopard-print thong over his stained jeans. Last night. I can smell the piss off him still.

'Grand bit of heat in that sun,' he says. He's glassy-eyed and staggering a bit.

'Timber. You're off somewhere nice?' I say.

He does a little dance on the street and people move away from him, including Nicky.

'I'll be in for my fried cheese on Monday. Fecking lovely shtuff,' he says. 'I'll never eat that Tesco sliced shit again.'

He tilts his head to the side and examines Nicky like a guard. 'Christ, you're fierce tall – that must be a pain in the neck.'

He cackles at his own joke and waltzes past us, swigging from his can. He doesn't remember a thing about last night and I envy him his obliteration of life. Nicky hops into a silver Astra and pulls off, wheels revving.

'Say it,' says Jade.

'Say what?' I'm locking the café door and panicking about whether I turned off the cooker, the coffee machine, the lights.

'You don't like him.'

I shrug. 'I don't know him.'

'He made you faint and I got the hate vibe from you.'

'Jade, seriously? He didn't make me faint. He's ... he seems OK.'

'But? I can hear a but in your voice.'

'What age is he?' We're walking up to the top of the town, where the graveyard overlooks us, clinging on to sheer rockface with grim determination.

'There it is. Same as the others. Age? Who fucking cares about age? Guys my age are toddlers, eejits who still have farting competitions. He's cool. Informed about women's rights. Fun. Who gives a fuck about age? And don't launch into all your brain development theories, all bullshit. Some people are just mature for their age. Like me.'

We turn right at Daley's pub and out the Lord's Cove road. The beach road. This is where the cool people hang out: the surfers, musicians, crafters, just generally cool people. We don't live there. Of course we don't. Dad would never fall for that. That'd be way too much fun. Nope. We live up a boreen with grass growing up the middle. I sneak a glance at Jade to see if her rant is over. Timber was right: the sun is blistering my head and my uncovered arms.

'He's twenty-five. I really like him.' Her voice is quiet. 'I don't want you to be all judgey, Saoirse.'

He's more than twenty-five and something is off with him but I swallow my words. Jade changes her partners as often as her hair colour.

'There's the little house on the prairie,' she says as we reach the cottage.

A work in progress, as Dad says. Dad's being kind to himself there. He loves to start stuff – tools out, new saws from Aldi, blocks ordered, dressed in what he thinks is builder's attire – but his enthusiasm never lasts more than a couple of days. His thing is the garden, the five acres of land that came with the cottage. He loves his polytunnels and his vegetable markets every other day and most of all he loves his chickens.

Two of them spot me and come clucking up the path.

'How are my lads? Did ye miss me?' I say, bending to let them peck my hand.

'Lads? Hens are female,' says Jade. 'This place is cuter than I remember.'

'That was March with the wind howling. Wuthering Heights.'

She lowers her hand to the chickens before I can stop her. They nip her so hard, the little feckers, they draw blood. I see my sister, Eva, standing at the window, phone in hand, face like a Russian hitwoman. Last night. The ear. Here we go.

It's dark. The hallway's cluttered with egg boxes, tons of them stacked in every available space. My chest tightens, I can feel it squeeze air from my lungs. I do the breathing thing that the counsellor taught me that never works.

Dad's in the kitchen, scrubbing a pot so hard I think it's going to disintegrate.

'Jade – I didn't recognise you – your hair is ...'

'Blue, John, and short. Do you like my undercut?'

Jade lifts her long fringe to show him. Aran comes into the kitchen and beams when he sees Jade.

'That's so cool, Jade, will you give me an undercut? Dad, can I? Can I?'

That's the longest sentence I've heard Aran say in months.

'You got taller, Aran,' says Jade. He smiles and stretches to full height.

Jade's being kind. Aran's twelve but looks way younger. Dad promised him a growth spurt that never came.

'You're staying for dinner, Jade, aren't you?' says Dad. 'How's your mother? The lads? All well?'

'Yep, no worry with them. They're all bonkers, though, but sure that's nothing new. Mam added a new job to her long list – her dream job she calls it – she's an usher at Thomond Park for the matches. She'd be bonkers too only for the rugby. I called out to your mother last week – I was on the doss from school, don't tell my mam.'

'You called to Nan? Why didn't you tell me?' I say.

'Telling you now, like.'

'How is she?' Dad stops his pot-scrubbing and has a big guilty head on him.

'She's wondering why ye never go back home,' says Jade, eyeing Dad.

'Ah, you know, the lads have school and the farm and all. And sure I ring her all the time. I've started a new project. I'll show you later. Saoirse, what'll we rustle up for our visitor?'

I stare at the contents of the fridge, while admiring Dad's diversion tactics. I didn't lick it off the stones. The fridge is jammed. Eggs, a lot of them. A knot of lettuces that look like they are reproducing themselves. Baby carrots. A huge white tub with gloop inside and a warning: 'Izzy Goat's first cheese – not for consumption'. I laugh at Dad and his little Post-it warnings and his cheesemaking efforts, which I think will follow the same path as the renovations.

'So – grub,' says Dad. 'Are you still a vegetarian, Saoirse?'

He asks this at least once a day, like I have the flu and it will run its course. I can hear Jade and Aran laughing.

'Dad ...'

'Only I got a nice bit of beef from Ryan's and I might make a stew. Eva loves a good stew.'

'Where is she?' says Jade, looking around the tiny kitchen as if she's hiding somewhere.

'Sulking,' says Aran. 'Sulking and moody as fuck ...'

'Language,' says Dad.

'And screaming for your head, Saoirse. She says you're bonkers and a vampire and everyone hates you in town and ...'

Aran's eyes are watering and he drops his head and wipes them on his T-shirt. He hates drama, it makes people see him. Notice him.

'I told him already – storm in a teacup – ye teenagers are always at it,' says Dad.

'Come on,' says Jade to me. 'Upstairs.'

In the hallway I try to do the stupid deep breathing again and wonder how counsellors get away with such shite. Eighty euro a pop to learn to breathe. Something you know as soon as you're born.

We go upstairs, an upstairs made for hobbits, and I pick up my guitar. I strum it and blink away stupid tears. Jade's quiet for once, stretched out on the bed, arms behind her head.

'She's taking her time,' says Jade.

'She's probably on her phone reporting my appearance to her coven of bitches,' I say.

'Why doesn't he come to Limerick? Your dad?'

I shrug and play the opening bars of an old Janis Ian song. Old songs are the best.

'You too, Saoirse. You avoid coming home too and sure you'll be in college there in a few months and you'll have to just get on with it. She'd have wanted that, your mam. Come up after the exams. You can stay in your nan's and we could, you know, go out and stuff and catch up with the lads and there's, like, this brilliant new open mic in The Fat Pig. I went with Nicky and you'd love it and –'

'I understand Dad. I know where he's coming from.'

'Yeah, but it's – I don't know – not a great idea, is it? Limerick is home, like.'

I stop strumming and watch her, eyes closed, blue hair on a white pillow. She looks childlike, beautiful, but in a raw, unconventional way, like somebody who wandered into my room from a surreal painting. I feel that fierce punch of jealousy and possession that I remember feeling since we were kids – when she talked to other girls – when boys liked her – when Nana's face lit up every time she saw her – the way Mam would say her name. She opens her eyes and grins at me.

'I'm dying of a hangover. Have you anything stashed here?' She gets up and rummages through my desk.

'Christ – all the Post-its and notes and all the fucking books? You've been eating the books, haven't you? Is that a real head – like is that what's in our brains?'

She picks up my phrenology head that Dad mistakenly thought I would love last Christmas.

'It's a phrenology head.'

'A what? Do I even want to know?'

'Phrenology is a pseudoscience where –'

'My hangover can't take this, Saoirse – brains are boring – any naggins stashed anywhere? I bet Eva has – is that her side of the room? Nicky wouldn't be able to stand up straight here. Ta-da!'

She whips out a half-full naggin from Eva's locker.

'Don't touch it – she's ready to kill me already.'

'I'll fill it with water. Don't worry.'

She takes a sip and shivers. 'Fuck. I needed that. Your books are staring at me, guilting me out, little bastards. Watch them.'

She throws a cushion at my desk.

'I am so fucked for these exams and do you know what, Saoirse – I don't care. Nicky says you don't need college to make money, he says he'll get me a job in one of his –'

'What happened to "Fuck the patriarchy"?'

She laughs. 'That's exactly what I'm doing. You said it yourself.'

She scans my photos on a pinboard over my desk. A life history in snapshots. Highlights. Images. Seconds. No context.

'I love this one of you and Finn. His curls are fucking amazing. I still don't get what happened between you.'

I examine the photo. Our smiles. The sea behind us. Hair salt-wet. Some of the gang in the background. A photo is the outside of something, and in the early days, that's what Finn and I saw in each other. Only the outside. That was enough last summer. It made me feel like I belonged. Like my new life fitted. It didn't.

'We called it a day,' I say. 'That's all,'

She eyes me, hand on hip. 'And?'

'And nothing. I wasn't in a place in my head for ... you know ... big relationships. I felt overwhelmed.'

'Jesus. Couldn't you just take the fun and have the ride and stop with all the self- analysis?' She takes another swig from the bottle. 'Fuck. It's like petrol. Tesco own brand, sixteen-year-olds have no taste.'

I want to tell her. Spill my guts to her like I would have two years ago, but now there's that space between us that can't be filled with Facetime and rushed visits. I want to tell her that I'm contagious and my broken bits seeped into Finn's and we were a perfect petri dish of misery. Instead I tune my guitar.

Footsteps pound up the stairs and I can nearly smell the anger and temper in those steps. Jade caps the naggin bottle and shoves it into the locker.

'Let the drama begin,' she says as Eva barges into the room.

She's standing in the doorway with a face like I'd just killed her pet dog.

'Hi, Eva,' Jade says.

'Why?' Eva's spearing me with her eyes. She's still holding her phone in her hand.

'You weren't there.'

'I didn't have to be. You fucking bit his ear off, you total weirdo.'

'Not his full ear, just a nip,' says Jade.

'What's wrong with you? Why can't you be just … just normal? The whole town's talking about it. I'm mortified, I am. You're just a complete gowl.'

Her voice is rising and she flicks her blond hair and pouts at me like she's practising for a selfie.

'You ruin everything. Your friends, Finn, everything. Selfish fucking bitch with your counselling – poor Saoirse. Poor Saoirse my hole.'

Her face is going pink under her false tan. Eva doesn't know how to handle non-confrontation. I glance at Jade, who looks like she's watching her favourite episode of *Schitt's Creek*.

'I'm asking Dad for my own room. I hate having to share with a weirdo,' she says, flouncing around like some cartoon teenager, checking her phone, stripping off her tracksuit and putting on more make-up. She is the superwoman of multitasking. Jade has covered her face with a cushion but I know she's laughing and I pick up my guitar and strum a nice depressing blues number. I know how to drive Eva mad. She plugs her phone into a speaker and some rapper I don't know screams his frustrations into the quiet West Clare evening. Eva always wins the torture wars.

4

Nicky's a big hit with Dad. Maybe it's an age thing. Or a car thing, because there's a major discussion about the reliability of Opel over any other make. I watch them pull away down the narrow boreen, Jade's blue head like a beacon in the front seat. I stand there for a while, listening to evening sounds. The cows in the field opposite have gathered in a stare group, waiting for me to feed them or sing or dance for them. I can hear a cuckoo somewhere. Bastard birds who couldn't be bothered making nests of their own. Imposters who win. I feel shaky and tired and wired all at the same time. At least Eva's gone to town and I don't have to deal with hitwoman vibes. I walk down to the far field, away from the cuckoo and the judgey cows.

Dad's working on more lettuces. Whole tunnels of them – we could keep the country in lettuce for years. He's in the biggest polytunnel, right at the bottom of the field. Izzy Goat has followed him in and is having a lettuce feast. Dad doesn't notice.

'Hi,' I say. I sit on an upturned rain barrel.

'Saoirse. How was work?'

'Grand. Joey's sound.'

'I don't know how he's paying you – he'll have to put a bit of meat on the menu if he wants to make a living.'

I smile and wonder if Dad ever takes his own advice? He was an accountant until the crash came and then he went a bit loopy. All back-to-the-earth talk and how consumerism consumed us all and how we should keep it simple. He could never work for 'Big Corporation' again. Mam dying made him worse. Which is all grand except when you force members of your family to live your dream, your ideal, your perfection. Sometimes I think we'll all just explode some day and Sunflower Cottage will be a blood bath on Sky News.

'More lettuce?'

'Yeah – and basil – there's going to be an awful shortage of basil next year. I feel it in my water. Hand me over that trowel.'

Dad feels a lot of things in his water and I know now that he will never predict the future, the weather, the next trend, the football results, what's for dinner.

'Feck off, Izzy! Did you leave that goat in?'

'She was here all the time.'

Dad glares at Izzy Goat. She has a stray piece of lettuce hanging from the corner of her mouth.

'That business last night. What happened?'

'It was just stupid, that's all, Dad. Nothing to worry about.'

'Eva said you bit somebody?'

'Eva's overdramatic. You know that.'

'She's a great girl, our Eva. She loves it here so she does,' he says, smiling at me.

I nod. Eva is Dad's success story. She's thrived here while Aran and I drowned. But I can't take away Dad's consolation prize. Even though I think she's a lighting bitch. Middle child, blessed with an easy personality, no pimples, a bit naïve, a bit stupid. Well able to down a naggin of vodka. She's perfect for Cloughmore. Dad needs every reassurance he can get because I hear him crying into his glass of Merlot at night. Lonely, fragile crying after holding it in all day.

'Come on, it's time,' he says. The goat and I follow him. We sit on a half-made swing seat, one of Dad's earlier DIY efforts. It doesn't swing and it has no back but it gives you the best view ever of the sunset. And there it is in blazing neon orange, little ribbons of cloud striping the sky around it. Dad breathes in – he'd do great with my counsellor. Izzy sits by his feet like a pet dog. I stretch out my legs and fold my arms like I'm watching a movie.

It's spectacular tonight and I instinctively check my pockets for my phone. To capture it. To take it and keep it on a pinboard in my bedroom instead of my head. No phone. I'll resurrect my ancient Nokia 3310. No notifications with that. No urge to fight the beep like it's some impatient omnipotent boss of your world. The sun does its thing and we stroll home through the fields. Dad's talking about basil again like it's the new potato of Ireland. We'll never go hungry because of basil and lettuce. We won't have a very varied or filling diet but we'll have loads to spare. There'll never be another famine.

Later, I take out my laptop and delete all my social media apps, resisting the urge to look at any. I throw my smashed phone into my locker and find the old Nokia, still perfect and one charge will last a whole week. Old SIM still intact. Indestructible. Nearly there. Study. Exams. Work for the summer and I'm out of here. I do a Jade and ignore the stack of Leaving Cert books and, instead, settle down with my latest book obsession – Ray Kurzweil, the Google director of engineering, who believes we will be able to upload our entire brains to computers within thirty years. Good old Ray, you have to like him, but more so the drugs he's on. I think if Ray from Google was here right this minute, he'd be rolling back on his little theories. Nothing like a dose of Cloughmore to syphon imagination from you. But still, I wonder what the likes of Joey or even Timber Hanley would make of Ray's ideas? Would they dismiss them out of hand? But didn't people dismiss the idea of mobile phones? It seems mad now but my nana told me about it. I love Nana and I know she's due one of her visits but she has zero filter and in our house you need many filters, probably armour and an electronic force field to even navigate dinner. Nana remembers when there were no mobile phones, music was only on vinyl and there were no remotes for the TV, that's if there even was a TV. Aran loves this story of people having to constantly pop up and down from the couch just to change the channel – if there *was* another channel. He always laughs at that bit.

So maybe Ray has a grain of truth mixed in there. Advances in technology aren't all silly. There's the cochlear implant, an implant attached to the brain's cochlear nerve, which electronically stimulates it to restore hearing to someone who's deaf. There should be a law about technological advances: they should only be funded and supported if they enhance human life. I pull out my laptop and go down a Google rabbit hole on the brain. I'm reading about brain mapping. It takes two years to map a fly's brain so mapping a human brain is a long way off. If we could create the wiring diagram of a brain and read the constant connection activity of all its neurons, could we then correct it? Say a person is depressed, schizophrenic, aggressive – could we just correct these issues?

Brains are complicated shit. The more I learn about them, the less I know. Maybe clinical psychology is not for me at all. I might be better off with a broader degree. Do I even want a degree? How are you supposed to know what you want to spend your life doing before you've done it and at eighteen? And Ray Google and his ilk only add to the complications. Mind uploading? Living digitally for ever? Who'd even want that? I'm liking the neuroscientists who argue against this, who say that the brain's dynamic complexity from which the human condition emerges – can't be replicated. You can't code intuition, aesthetic beauty, love, hate, happiness, sadness, grief, loneliness.

The question is: what defines a person? What makes us human? Now I'm down another Google rabbit hole in a maze of rabbit holes. Some scientists claim that the mind is just a complex computer whose function depends on electrochemical processes. They say that if we can sufficiently emulate the neural networks of the brain, it's natural that intelligence and consciousness follow. I hate them but I seek them out now too like scary movies. I want to be convinced that it's all nonsense but a tiny part of me is fascinated by it. There are 'grinders' – guerrilla scientists – in labs across the world experimenting in these fields already and experimenting on themselves in the process. Mad, but Isaac Newton did exactly that, so not so crazy after all.

It must be great to be Eva in the world. She wants to be a make-up artist. Or a nail technician. She could be either, right now, and never have to spend another day at school. She's not like Aran or me, though, she loves school. Loves the drama and the pals and the covens and knots that need to be negotiated. She doesn't give one fuck about how the brain works and maybe she's right. But brains are fascinating yokes all the same.

I'm pulled away from brain thoughts by the sound of a car outside. An unusual sound here at any time of the day but especially at night.

'Saoirse? Dylan's here,' Dad shouts from downstairs.

Fuck. He's the last person I want to see while trying to shake last night out of my system. Maybe I could feign sleep?

'Saoirse? It's important.' Dad again, giving me zero choice.

I check myself in the mirror and want to kick myself for doing it. I go downstairs and Dylan and Dad are squashed against the egg boxes in the tiny hallway.

'Dylan. Hi. What's up?' Dad moves discreetly into the kitchen. I'm thinking the worst – Cian's ear fell off or Jade and Nicky crashed or Eva? Jesus, something happened to Eva. Dylan's eyes are red and his face is blotchy, swollen. 'What? What's wrong, Dylan?'

'I tried to ring you all evening. I left messages, I tried to –'

'Tell me – is it Eva? Did something happen to Eva?'

'It's … it's Finn. He's missing since this morning and there are search parties out and I tried to contact you and –'

'This morning? He could be anywhere – Ennis – he has friends there, loads of them – or Lisdoon or …' I stop to savour the fact that it's not Eva and hate myself for it.

He shakes his head. 'The guards have been told and the sea rescue. His phone is at home.'

'Are they still searching?'

'No. Called it off just now. They're organising a huge search in the morning. Look, I've to go back – Mam's waiting outside.'

'Hang on – I want to come. I want to search too. In the morning.'

Dylan's doing the thing lads do so they won't cry, where their face becomes mobile and stretched. I want to hug him but it feels wrong.

'We'll pick you up. Around 4.30?'

I want to tell him that Finn'll be grand – that he'll arrive home langers in the middle of the night, that he'll be down to Circle K for his breakfast roll when he surfaces at lunchtime, that he's safe. That anything else is not possible. But I know that's all a pile of lies. A heap of horseshit.

'Thanks,' I say, like a pure gowl. 'I'll text you my number. My own phone ... my phone is broken.'

He nods and leaves but turns back and leans his head on my shoulder and I want to cry hard now. I still can't hug him. Instead I touch his back, like an acquaintance would, a light stroke between his shoulder blades. It feels like burn.

*   *   *

Dad's packing a bag for me. Flask, sandwiches, flashlights, fruit. It's like I'm going on a holiday, a little camping trip. Eva's in bed, obviously drunk, or she'd have come into the kitchen for the drama. Aran's tailing Dad and I know he's heard us talking. This tiny house does not accommodate privacy or whispered conversations. Everybody knows everything. Dad's also saying all the right things. The platitudes we tell ourselves when shit happens. I hug him goodnight while he's still in mid-sentence. He kisses the top of my head and hugs me so hard it hurts.

I can smell the alcohol as soon as I open the bedroom door. She's lying on her back and moonlight spills into the room from the skylight. She has mascara rings under her eyes and snores lightly. I climb into bed and pull the duvet over my head to block out the moon and the snoring and the world.

I told you the sky is falling down. I told you, Mam.

5

Dawn is breaking over the headland as we reach the meeting point – the GAA pitch at the far side of Cloughbeg, which is a tiny fishing village on the edge of the sea. Dylan's mam parks up and she touches his hand as she gets out of the car. Dylan sits in silence, unmoving, watching as the crowds gather and are split into groups.

'Are you OK?' The instant I say it I know it's the stupidest thing.

He shakes his head.

'Do you ... do you want to just wait here? I'll stay here ... I mean ... I'll stay if you want me to.'

Another shake of the head and I don't know if that means yes or no. I grab my backpack and climb out of the car and he's right behind me as I walk towards the search organisers. Megan, Kate and Cian are huddled in a group and I do a swift detour to avoid them. Dylan follows me. I can feel Megan's eyes on me, lasers that see through bodies and trees. Voices are low and hushed, like Mass whispers.

I'm standing right beside Finn's mother, Dee, and when she sees me she pulls me close and hugs me. I fight back tears and she's whispering in my ear but none of it makes sense in my head. And somehow Megan is beside us, pulling her mother away from me and lasering me again with those eyes, eyes that say, *This is on you, this is your fault.* Dee squeezes my hand as she leaves. That squeeze is everything in the moment.

We break into groups and fan out across the cliff fields and the glows from the flashlights look like fallen-down stars. The grass is dew-damp and the air salt-laden. Banks of fog stripe the horizon and blue sky peeps out as the sun rises. A beautiful day promised, and none of us should be here, doing this. Dylan is still silent, examining the ground like it's going to give him answers, some clue about his friend that will quiet all the questions.

'Where would he go, Saoirse? Where would he go if he ... you know ... if he was going to do it?' he says.

'Jesus, Dylan, I don't know. Let's not jump to any conclusions. I still think he might turn up, you know. He might be anywhere and just going off grid for a while or maybe he has one of his giant hangovers and is clearing his head and ...'

He stops and looks at me. 'He took his bike. Nobody has seen him since yesterday morning. No phone. You're the science woman. The brain-facts woman. Do the sums.'

He sees something in the grass and hunches down to examine it. I do too and our heads touch as Dylan pokes the item with his flashlight. It's an old plastic water bottle, moss greening its surface, a beetle family scurrying inside.

'He took his bike,' he says again. I nod, my face inches from his. 'Where would he go?'

I feel like I'm failing an exam but it's not something Finn and I chatted about when we were together. *Where would you choose to kill yourself? To take your own life? To die by choice?*

'I don't know. You're his closest friend, where do *you* think he is?' My voice is shaky and hoarse. Dylan stands up and puts his flashlight away. The light is luminous now, finding its way into crevices and creeks and through blades of grass.

'He's alive, Saoirse. I feel it. I just know he didn't ... wouldn't ... not with the county final coming up and the Leaving Cert and ... he just wouldn't ...'

He walks ahead of me, trying to catch up with the search party. A chopper whirs out at sea, hovering and retracing its path. If you live by the coast you learn to know that sound, that reminder that the sea takes as well as gives. He's gone. That's what I feel in my water as Dad would say. Finn is gone.

* * *

They find his bike by the cliffs. He even locked it. Tourists throng the cliff path and phones are whipped out to take videos of the search chopper hovering over the sea. They don't know what it is, just that it's a helicopter, bright red, close to the dramatic cliff face. There's a buzz of excitement over the bike. Over the fact that he locked it, and Dee, Finn's mother, is smiling and hugging Megan and the hope stabs me. Steals the air in my lungs. I can feel it from

52

Dylan too, that tiny light of optimism as we walk the cliff path towards White Shore.

'I told you he's OK,' he says. 'He's gone off on one of his trips. Probably brought his tent. He's been doing that since ... since ye split up. Just takes himself off like Bear Grylls. He left the bike at the cliffs so he could go off on a hike. I mean, you can't hike over the rocks out here on a bike.'

Dylan's talking like Jade, a head spew, a live thought process, and I let it play out. Dissociate. It's a white-hot blistering day now. Leaving Cert weather. The sea to our left is calm and glassy and still. Innocent. Harmless. Pretty. The search party is a long snake weaving across stone and rock. I'm watching the helicopter as it combs land from the sky. It stops a little away, purring above White Shore. Dylan's voice is white noise, like words under water that can't climb for air. The search party hope is still there, in their step, in their gait, and I fixate on the chopper and I know.

We round the bend of cliff that offers the most surreal view of White Shore, and though I've been here loads, it always surprises me. Makes me appreciate living here. It's a tiny white sandy cove, the white sand making the water look turquoise. It's like a tiny bit of Barbados in West Clare. The chopper has dropped low and I hear a power boat in the distance and the murmur around me is hope again. We make our way down steep steps carved into the cliff face. A few families are scattered about, availing of the car park on the hilltop. I fixate on two children, in red polka dot swimsuits. Twins. Pink buckets. Green shovels. They're digging in the sand and throwing lumps of it onto the plaid blanket beside them. Their mother is reading a book, and the father's arm is static, mid-reach in a wicker basket. I know what he's looking at. I know already, but I keep my eyes on the twins, and then the next family, a dad with a string of energetic boys fighting over a crab captured in a Chivers jam jar of water. Its claws scrape the jar in a futile effort to escape.

He's at the very end of the cove, around a sandy corner, behind a worn-down sea stack. Search and Rescue have drawn up and are shouting at us to move away, to stay where we are, to get out of here. I can still feel the hope from Dylan as he quickens his step and there he is. Finn. Black curls against white sand, green ringlets of seaweed knitted into his hair. White-grey skin. Gold GAA jersey, blue denims. Bare feet. Adidas backpack on his shoulders. Body foetal but face turned to the sun. The noise around me is a glug of sounds, crying, shouting. A paramedic is giving CPR to Finn and I want to push him off and just hold Finn in my arms and tell him it'll be OK. His navy Superdry hoodie is folded neatly on the shoreline, well out of the way of the tide. His Vans rest on top with his watch, a cheap one I'd given him for Christmas. His socks are folded into each other and stuffed into one shoe.

The paramedic stops and I feel relief that they're finally going to leave his body alone and then he starts up again. *One. Two. Three. One. Two. Three.* Dylan has grabbed my hand and squeezes it hard and tight like it's going to help some-how. The paramedic stops and just drops his head. Defeat.

Another takes the backpack, skewed to Finn's side. It's full of rocks and they spill onto white sand like an ancient god's fossilised tears.

*　　*　　*

They've gathered at the GAA pitch. Neighbours, friends, Eva and her coven, Dad and Aran. Faces blur into each other as I get out of the car and all I can see and hear are snatches of colour and voices all mashed together in a hum. A human murmuration. Dylan hasn't said a word since the beach. Not a single word, grunt, cry. Nothing. On the way back, Dylan's mother tried to fill the car with comfort words and phrases but they banged off the car windows and dropped to the floor like trapped flies. Useless.

I don't know what to do. Dylan and Megan are hugging and crying and I'm standing here like a complete gowl. The others come over and form a circle with Dylan and Megan. A huddle, like in a football match. Me on the sidelines. Or the sin bin. And then Dad's here with his arms around me and the lovely smell of him, soap and chicken shit, and Aran's doing my crying for me.

'Do you want to stay with your friends, Saoirse? I can come back and collect you later or you can have the car – sure they're all driving here on their provisional licences and –'

'I want to go home.' I say this as I watch the huddle grow bigger. Classmates and teammates summoned, space made for them. Eva and her coven drawn in. I catch Megan's eyes for an instant, deadlier than Eva's Russian hitwoman stare. I can feel the hate like it's a physical connection. We walk to the car as the sun goldens the pitch, the goalposts tall and white in yellowed fading light. Aran slips his hand into mine and sits in the back with me, wet eyes patching dark stains on my sleeve. I want to comfort him, but we've been here before and he knows that words are just words.

'Are ye hungry? I'll stop at Manny's for chips,' Dad says, as he drives the narrow road towards town. ''Tis an awful business altogether. Very sad.' His words are more useless flies locked in a car. But he keeps going. Keeps trying to fill the space between.

'Terrible thing to happen. So young. Everything going for him, great footballer too ...'

'Dad. Stop.'

'I'm just trying to help, Saoirse, I'm only trying to –'

'Please. Just stop.'

'OK, it's just ... it's just so hard, that's all. For you. It's just so hard ...'

His voice chokes up and I can see him in the mirror, doing that Dylan thing with his face, stretching it so he won't cry. Aran is glued to me, and he feels smaller, younger.

We pull up outside Manny's as the last pink light dips in the sky. I have a low, tight pain in my head and I wish I could wipe it like a hard drive, just dump all the memory strands that I don't want or like into the recycle bin. Delete all.

'Do you want to go in, Saoirse? Manny's ...'

'No.'

'Am … OK. What'll you have? Are you still a vegetarian?'

'Yes, Dad. Garlic chip. Burger and chip for Aran.'

'Grand so. Anything else?'

Dad climbs out of the car, knowing the answer already. I wish I had my headphones so that I could fill my head with noise. Loud noise. Instead, I pick at my fingers until they bleed.

'Saoirse.' Aran doesn't lift his head from my arm, so his voice is muffled.

'Yep.'

Sniffles. Snot dripping on my arm. 'Why?'

'Why what?' I know what he means, though.

'Why did Finn … like … do that?'

Jesus Christ. How do you answer that?

'I don't know, Aran. People get sad sometimes and …' My words swirl around the car and slip out the window. Useless words. Lies.

'Yeah but … but … I get sad and I didn't do that and it's so not fair, cos, like, Mam wanted to be alive, not dead, and he just … did that thing and … it's not fair …'

'I know. It's not fair,' I say, and he buries his head deeper into the crook of my arm.

There's a knock on the window and Manny's there, in his white apron, dark skin blotched with sweat. He's opening the door and before he can I'm out and throwing myself into his arms and the tears come only then, mixed with chip-fat smells and Manny's tight hug.

He doesn't say anything, not one word. He just holds me and I cry like I'd forgotten how and the muscle memory just kicked back in. We stand there on Main Street, in the still dusk, like we are caught in time.

'Manny ... Manny ... the chip pans are making a weird noise – like they're going on fire,' says Dad from the doorway of the chipper.

'I say one thing, Saoirse, one thing,' says Manny. 'Not your fault. Nobody's fault.'

He pulls away and runs into the shop. I lean against the car window, Aran's ghost-face watching me from the car. *Not your fault.* I wish that was true. It is my fault. All of it.

6

This waiting room. There are posters on the wall, sunsets and seas and trite quotes about how the dark times will pass and how it's OK not to be OK. I hate that one the most. They have that up in the common room in the convent. Anybody who's not OK knows this as the biggest lie. There's a sunset poster right in front of me, at eye level. Lovely sunset, the usual, with the words *You are allowed to be sad.* Another lie. You're not allowed to be sad. People have no tolerance for sad. You can be Insta sad – sad because you saw pictures of dying refugees or abandoned puppies. You can't be ongoing sad. You can't be scared or anxious or upset. And you can't be suicidal until it's too late. These are negative things and people hate negative. So what happens when you can't hide sad any more?

Malcolm, my so-called therapist, has hit the jackpot. We are all offered a counselling session before the funeral and Malcom is the only therapist in town. Some people have opted to go to Ennis, but I reckon I'm better off with the devil I know. The Clancy twins come into the waiting room, heads down, mortified, like they're doing something illegal. I watch them, enjoying their embarrassment. They look through me like I'm glass. My palms begin to sweat and I'm wondering if new rumours have erupted. Fuck them. I stare them down and force them to look away in unison. Will they have twin counselling too and is it two for the price of one? I hum a Joni Mitchell oldie and it makes the twins squirm. It also makes my palms stop sweating.

'Saoirse?'

'Yep.' I jump up and wonder if he caught me humming to myself. I always feel like I have to behave for Malcolm, just in case he thinks I'm bonkers.

'Come on in,' he says. I follow him into his treatment room, an extension onto his bungalow on the fringes of town. There's a salt lamp in the corner and candles. Malcom likes a good candle. The smell of sandalwood and lilies makes me feel sick. There is a low couch facing his desk. I sit opposite him and already feel like we are in a duel.

'How have you been? Let's see – three weeks since I last saw you?'

'Yep.' I'm glad of a question I can answer.

'So, how are you feeling after ... after Saturday's events?'

Oh, fucking great. Here we go. Finn's death is an event. Malcolm will find a way to relate everything back to my mother because he has a weird Freudian fixation. My stomach rumbles like Mount Etna. I hope he doesn't hear it.

'OK. Sad.'

'I hear you, Saoirse, and I feel your pain.'

No, you fucking don't, Malcolm. You have no idea of my pain. None.

'You are grieving, Saoirse, and it brings up pain associated with your mother's death.'

He leans back on his swivel chair, folds his arms across his chest and looks at me like he's delivered an encryption key to unlock world peace. The air is thick with silence. I can see him eyeing my bleeding skinned fingers.

'Look, Saoirse. You need to talk about Finn Ryan. He was your boyfriend ...'

'Ex.' My voice is whispery.

'Ex. Whatever. This is a huge shock and you're ... well ... fragile.' He's swivelling slightly, hands now on the desk in front of him.

I shrug. *Fuck off, Malcolm, with your DIY therapy. Stating the obvious.*

'I'd like us to talk about avoidance.'

I wish I could avoid you, Malcolm.

'Grand,' I say, examining my nails.

'I hear you, Saoirse.'

I'm the only other person in the room so, yeah, no-brainer there, Malcolm.

He checks his notes from our last session. Shakes his head like I'm a hopeless case.

'Death by suicide is very hard for those left behind.'

No shit, Malcolm. And actually, death by any means is hard for those left behind, you absolute gowl.

'We tend to blame ourselves, to examine every conversation, to look for a cause. We spoke about Finn at your last session.'

He looks at me like he's asked me a question. I nod. *You spoke about him, Malcolm.*

'What I mean is ...'

He looks away towards the monitor on his desk and I wonder if he's Googled today's subject matter before these back-to-back sessions with Finn's circle of friends and peers.

'Disenfranchised grief.' He smiles, but it looks like he's congratulating himself for coming up with a psychobabble term. 'Well, Finn was your ex-boyfriend, and you may face implications that you have less of a right to mourn him.'

Nail on the head there, Malcolm. I have no right to mourn him. If only you knew.

'Saoirse. It's normal to grieve the loss of anyone you had a meaningful relationship with. That includes your mother.'

Can we just talk about Finn, Malcolm?

'Saoirse? How do you feel about that?'

About what, Malcolm? I feel like shit about everything. I feel guilty and sad and weird and when I'm outside, in a group, everybody sounds like they're under water and they speak gluggy fish language and I want to go home.

'I'm sad,' I say just to shut him up.

He smiles. Correct answer.

'You see, with Finn, because you finished the relationship, people probably won't expect you to grieve and therefore won't support you. They may suggest that you shouldn't feel 'that sad' because you finished with him. By internalising these messages, you effectively disenfranchise your own grief, which can lead to difficulty working through the ... distress.'

I drop my head and blink away tears. I know Malcolm got this from Wiki but all I see in my head is the football huddle on the GAA pitch and me outside it. Excluded. I'm also thinking that maybe Megan was in here before me and filled his head with shit about me.

'A ritual may help.'

I have this image in my head of witches and spells. Sabrina style.

'Write a letter to Finn. A eulogy. Say all of the things you feel, even bad things.'

'Good idea,' I say, throwing him a bone.

He nods. I know by his head that Dad has been in his ear. I can smell it off him. 'Do you think that might be something that will help?' His eyebrows twitch upwards. He'd be useless at poker.

I focus now on the pictures above Malcolm's head. There's his degree in an expensive frame but it's not a degree. I Googled it after our first meeting. He's a psychotherapist. He probably did an online course and set himself up with candles and a *Psychotherapy for Dummies* handbook for the tough cases.

'Saoirse? Did you hear me?'

'Yep.'

'Have you talked to your friends about Finn?'

'No.'

'Saoirse, I feel your pain.'

'Yep.' I've moved on to examining the family portrait above Malcolm's right ear. A younger Malcolm with hair, his tiny wife, two smiley boys with red hair and matching freckles.

'You know, Saoirse, you can't avoid grieving.'

This time I look straight at him, at his long thin face, his grey bit of a beard, his blue liquid eyes. My fists are balls of sweat and my lungs are doing their vice-grip trick. I want to leave, just get up and give him the finger and walk out for ever, but that'll make everything worse. I know it's easier to sweat out the hour, to try to make this man feel like he's helping me. I wipe my hands on my jeans and suck air into my chest. I can do this. I have been doing it for weeks.

'I know. I just need time.' The words curdle on my tongue like bad milk.

'Huh huh.'

He nods and I know that 'huh huh' means continue. I want to tell him about neurons and Google Ray and all the stuff I'm reading but I know Malcolm. He'll read all sorts of nonsense into it. He'll call it avoidance. I try to think of another therapy bone I could throw him. Zero.

'Saoirse? You're doing so well. What are you avoiding in this moment? In this grieving moment? Shall we make a list?'

For fuck sake. Yep, we'll make a list and go off to SuperValu with it. Can I have some friends, an undead ex, a time machine so I can undo stuff, a magic drink to stop me thinking and a muffin please and here's my SuperValu loyalty card.

'That sounds good.'

'Lists are great to focus on the important issues. Let's see – let's think of things that you've been avoiding since Saturday's events ... any suggestions?'

I shrug. I don't know what he's looking for. It's like the Leaving Cert when you get a topic you've studied for, but they twist the question.

'You haven't grieved with your friends?'

I shake my head. The vice-grip pinches my chest. He must be the only person in Cloughmore who hasn't heard that I bit Cian Burke's ear off.

'Have you talked to your family?'

Another shake of my head. I'm failing this exam. 'My friend from Limerick is coming for the funeral. Jade. My friend, Jade.'

'Good, good, good, that's more like it.'

He folds his arms across his lap and leans towards me. I can smell mint and pesto.

'Saoirse. You're a smart girl. You will get through this. It's hard for all of you, what with the exams next week, but they've arranged a room for me in the school – I will be on hand for the duration.'

I nod.

'Saoirse. How are the blackouts?'

Blackouts? He's calling having naps in the middle of class blackouts? He should get his money back from the DIY online course.

'Gone.'

'Good, good, good. I note that the doctor prescribed you anti-depressants. How is that going?'

'Good.'

I'm lying, Malcolm, you gowl.

His little alarm bell goes and I'm on my feet and out the door while he's saying goodbye. The Clancy twins have conquered their territory and snigger and loud-whisper as I pass. *There she is now. The Vampire of Cloughmore. Hahaha.* Outside on the street I walk uptown, anger spitting inside me. Anger at myself, at Finn, but also Malcolm, with his quick fixes and two-euro solutions. I break into a run, my bag slapping against my thighs. I veer onto the road to avoid the nosey stares and a part of me wishes I was naked, give them something to really talk about. I hate this town, this claustrophobic, choking town, where I can't get a decent lungful of air. It's just one street, but it feels smaller. This town is the vampire. Not me.

7

Eva's in full wake mode, like Finn was her closest friend or even her ex. Herself and her coven are on the wake circuit, different houses, same clichés and tears, always managing to keep their mascara intact. I can imagine already the shit going down on social media. The tributes to him. The #bekinds and the #bestrongs and the absolute bullshit that they carry on with. Flowers out at White Shore – Insta-perfect pictures of a dead lad's life. The scurry for old photos that include him, the regurgitated conversations and jokes that they may or may not have shared with him. Gowls.

I'm list-making again. Malcolm would be delighted, but he doesn't know that I've been doing this since Mam got sick. He also doesn't know that it's not a good sign.

Things I know. Finn is dead. He's lying in Canty's morgue on Bridge Street in his best suit from his brother's wedding last year. The town is in mourning. Dylan hasn't been in touch. We all still have to sit the Leaving Cert. It's an even more pointless

exam now. The sun is still shining and Malcolm is still a gowl.
Nana's coming today. Jade is coming tomorrow.

Eulogies. Malcolm and his little ritual suggestion. I wrote one this morning. Ripped it up. Wrote another one. Each eulogy started off great and then wandered into truth. Malcolm's wrong again. You can't diss a dead lad. You just can't. I'm staring at my books on the desk, at the colour-coded Post-it notes, the pinned-up study plan. I take a marker and black out the days I will miss. Four. Maybe five? Is that enough for grieving? For Finn?

*   *   *

Nana fills the house with energy and noise and the ingredients for many gin and tonics. We're having dinner, all of us, including Eva, who has adopted the persona of a war widow who just got the telegram. Nana's voice is floating like a warm throw over all of us but Eva's annoying the shit out of me with the drama. I want to grab her painted face and say, *You didn't even fucking know him*, but instead I give her Russian hitwoman looks over the mound of lettuce salad.

'I never told ye, lads. I never told ye about Archie Cat,' Nana says, not wanting a lull in the conversation in case myself and Eva go for each other.

'Missing, he is. Missing almost a full week.' Her eyes fill with tears and I reckon she's been on the gin since lunch time.

'Archie always does that,' says Aran.

Nana shakes her head. 'It's different this time. I wasn't

going to say anything over ... well ... over poor Finn – it didn't seem right, like – but I can't keep it in any more. Are you listening to me, John?'

Dad nods but I think he tuned out about three gins ago.

Nana pauses for effect. 'Do you know that wan who lives three doors down? 'Twas her, I know it was.'

We've all bought into the story now, even Eva.

'You remember her, John, from when you were small? The wan that used to take in your footballs and never give them back?'

'The ex-nun?' says Dad.

'Her. Crabby auld bitch. She took an awful set against Archie – said he was shitting in her flowerpots. I says to her, I says, "How do you know it was my Archie? Did you do a DNA test on the shit?" Cheek of her. You'd swear Archie was the only cat in Thomondgate and her going around like she's CSI Limerick – I mean, she knows everything about everyone and their cats.'

Nana stops to gulp her drink. She's on a roll now. 'I saw her the day Archie disappeared. Acting funny like. Went off for a spin in the morning. That Micra hasn't been for a spin since Joe Dolan died and she'd an awful smug smile on her face when she met me in Tesco. She knew something. Bitch. She took him.'

Nana starts to cry. Dad pats her hand. Aran's waiting for the next instalment. I'm wondering if Nana's making all of this up to distract me from Finn.

'She took him, I know she did,' she says. 'Couldn't stand the sight of my Archie, told me once that black cats are bad luck – I mean she's an ex-nun, like, and she comes out with this. Bloody witch more like.'

The tears start up again and Dad's consoling her while Eva sneaks off for another chief mourner's round of the houses.

'He'll turn up, Nan,' I say. 'He's always going off on adventures.'

She shakes her head. 'Not for this long and it's the way that wan looks at me – like she has something over me. I've a good mind to say it to her.'

'That's not a good idea,' Dad says. 'You've no proof or anything, Mam.'

'She had no proof about the cat shit but had no trouble knocking on my door in the middle of *A Place in the Sun*. Is there any more steak? Sorry, Saoirse, I know you're a vegetinarian or vegan or something but I loves my meat.'

Dad rushes off in search of meat. Nana reaches across the table and grips my hand tight.

'You'll be fine, Saoirse. 'Tis fierce sad. No rhyme or reason to it. Sure we're the same back home with that bloody river. It has an awful draw to it altogether if you're ... you know ... in that frame of mind. I dread the sound of that helicopter and the way it hovers over the water. Your grandfather used to say 'twas the sound of death.'

I don't know if it's the mention of Granda or Finn or all of it, but I'm crying into my barely touched risotto. Aran takes this as permission to cry too so that when Dad comes back with the steak, we're all crying into our half-eaten dinners.

* * *

His coffin is simple. He'd have wanted that. I feel it should be raining. Instead, it's a beautiful late spring day. The birds in the graveyard compete with each other to sing. That kind of day. I can hear them, every single note, but everybody else sounds like they are submerged. This new fish-speak has spread since the day we found Finn. Dad says I'm blocking out the noise so that I can grieve. I think it's another spoke in my madness wheel. Dylan's here, flanked by two perfect parents. There is a gaping brown hole where Finn will lie soon between us. Like a moat. I can feel the weight of Dad's arm. I'm swimming in sadness. Nana has dressed like she's going to the opening of a play and Eva like she's going to a teen Energiser disco. Aran's welded to my side – my dress has a shiny new patch of snot. Jade is a no-show. An excuse text about car trouble followed by emojis that don't show up on an old Nokia.

The priest's voice glugs some kind of prayer. I want to laugh at how he sounds and looks, sweltering in his flowing robes and fish speaking. Dylan has his head bent and his mother's whispering to him. Patting him on the sleeve of his suit jacket. I recognise all the faces. School, town, café, shops, pharmacy. That's a small town for you. Everybody is recognisable. Timber has managed to clean up for the occasion, his leathery wrinkled face is clean shaven. He has the solemn funeral protocol down to a fine art.

71

The priest finishes and sprinkles the coffin. They begin to lower it and Timber plays a soft tune on a tin whistle. It becomes the only sound I can hear, lonely and plaintive in bright sun.

People begin to move away. They've done their duty. Served their time. There are sandwiches to eat and pints to drink. I touch the necklace that Finn gave me for my birthday. Silver with a delicate Celtic love knot. It's the first time I've worn it. I turn away as I see Dylan approach me, his parents hovering in the background.

'Hey.'

I can hear him. No glugging.

'I ... I'm sorry I didn't get to see you since ... you know. I messaged a few times but ... I thought you might need your space and stuff and ...'

I nod but I can't look at him. If I do, I'll think he's armour and I'll fall into him and make my shit his. I have a habit of that. 'Thank you.'

'Look, do you want to get a drink or something?' Dylan's reaching an arm towards me as he says this.

I step away. 'No. I'm fine.'

'I ... we need to talk.'

'Why?' I look at him now, straight into his eyes.

'About ... you know ... you know what I mean.'

'There's nothing to say, Dylan.'

He shrugs. He touches my arm, just for a second, and I almost break then, I almost hurl myself at him and comfort myself in him.

'See ya,' I say and walk towards Dad.

Things I know. There's no armour for sad.

I don't look back, but I know if I do I'll see the tight premier-league huddle at the graveside, the people in Finn's life. Dad's like a centurion, waiting by the exit with Nana and Aran. Big worried head on him because he read an article about copycat suicides. We walk towards the car, Nana struggling on the gravel in her black shiny heels.

'Saoirse. I'm here,' a voice yells from the road behind us.

I look back and there's Jade, all Goth in a black tulle dress and flowery Doc Martens and mad blue hair. She'd be late for her own funeral.

8

We're sitting in Crowe's on Main Street. It prides itself as a 'boutique townhouse' but it's more like a B and B with wine. Jade's at the bar, flirting with the barwoman. I can hear her flirty laugh. She has a special laugh for every occasion. The others have gone to The Cascades. I wasn't asked – not that I'd go. I'm sure Eva is there, representing the family, tears on tap and a naggin of vodka in her handbag.

'I got free shots,' says Jade, laying a tray laden with drinks and Taytos on the shaky round table. 'Push over, will you?'

She hands me a shot, winks at me and downs her own. I sip mine. It's putrid.

'Here – give it to me,' she says, and throws that one back too. 'Christ – the fucking day I had already, like. I fought with Mam over the lads leaving their shit everywhere and expecting anyone with a vagina to pick it up and then Nicky – we had our first fight. I mean, he pretends the car is fucked cos he didn't want to drive me here and then fucks off in it five minutes later. Bastard. And ... hey ...'

She reaches for me and pulls me into her and I have a little cry on her shoulder and hope I am not doing an Aran and leaving snot everywhere.

'It'll be OK, Saoirse, I promise,' she says. 'It's still shit, though – all of it.'

'They all hate me. Like it's my fault or something. Like I drove him to it ...'

Jade pulls away from me, wipes my eyes with her sleeve. 'Stop it. Just stop, Saoirse. It's nobody's fault. Fuck sake. You don't know what goes on in someone's head or their life. And fuck them. Told ya – didn't I? Megan? Kate? Dylan? It's exactly like the cool kids in Limerick – remember in school? The ones we laughed about? They're not your people, hun – never will be.'

She takes a slug from her pint, followed by a fistful of crisps. The barwoman comes over with two more shots. Jade admires her as she sashays away. I feel like I'm eavesdropping.

'The cool wans are lethal. They're the Darkness into Light wans – know what I mean? Up for the dawn walk with their candles and their photos and they'd turn away if you were hanging off Sarsfield Bridge. It's like an outing for do-gooders so they can tell the world how great they are, like.'

I love the sound of Jade's voice – so much more reassuring than Malcolm's. I knock back my shot and reach for my pint.

'That's my woman. G'wan, our Saoirse. Fuck them. They blocked me on everything, you know. Snapchat. Insta. Dumb Facebook. TikTok. They like to keep their bitch parties private. Air-kissing me last Friday night at the beach. Gowls.'

'What did he say? That night? What did ye talk about?'

Jade fiddles with her eyebrow piercing, which is a sure sign that I'll get an edited version of events. She takes a slug of Guinness. Another handful of crisps.

'Jade?'

'Look – we were all langers. Finn was … was grand. We talked about you – just general stuff, you know – how you were doing, how you have the best singing voice ever – he said that, not me – and how you never really know people.'

'What did that mean?'

Jade rolls her piercing around again. 'Dunno. Bit too deep for me, I was on the lash, like – so I asked him about college – you know. He said he was taking a year out …'

'I didn't know that.'

'Yeah … well … then Kate came over, throwing shapes at him, so I got up and walked away. That's it really.'

'Is it, though?'

'Yeah, it is. And don't go down that fucking road, Saoirse.'

'What fucking road? I want to know what was going on that night. That's all. Did he … did he take anything?'

'Like what? What are you saying?'

'Drugs – molly. You know.'

Jade laughs. 'Pure expert, I am. Bit insulted now, like – I know what you're really saying.'

'I'm just –'

'No. Be straight with me. You're saying we gave him molly. That's what you're saying. That we killed him. Fuck off, Saoirse.'

'I just want to know what happened. You were there. I wasn't.'

'Why don't you ask Golden Boy? He was there too – chatting with Finn all night – or is that too close to the bone for you?'

My hands are sweaty and leave wet prints on the table. My chest feels like somebody in lead boots is jumping on it. Pounding and squeezing the air out of me.

'Saoirse. It wasn't your fault. You'll crack up if you start blaming yourself.' She reaches across and grips my hand. 'Are you listening to me? It wasn't your fault. You did the same thing when your mam died – remember? Blaming the doctors, the chemo, your dad. Sometimes shit happens and there's no reason at all. Life is a dick.'

I nod. I feel too shaky to speak. She's saying what I want to hear but there's stuff being unsaid too. I can feel it.

'OK?'

Another nod from me.

'Slug that back. I need to catch the last bus. Nicky's texting and apologising and all, even though it was my fault. There's a gig in The Fat Pig tonight.'

'I thought you were rushing home to study,' I say, trying to lighten the mood.

'You're joking, right? I am so fucked and Mam's, like, telling everyone that I'm off to college – the first in the family. Jesus, the expectations, I swear. And the lads can do what they like.' She drains her glass and waves at the barwoman.

Outside, it's climate-change hot, a tar-melting scorcher of a day and the town feels sleepier than usual. We walk to the bus stop, Jade with an arm wrapped around my waist. 'Come with me,' she says. 'Come to Limerick. Fuck it – come on, like. The break'll do you good.'

The bus is already there, the driver leaning against the wall, having a smoke. I'm half-tempted to go, but I know I'm shaky. I know the signs and it never mixes well with crowds.

'I can't – Nana's at home and ...'

'Study. I know you well, Saoirse – always useless at skiving off.'

She kneels to pat an old Labrador in the doorway of a long-closed chemist's shop. Her black tulle skirt pools around her and she bobs her blue head up and down as she talks to the dog. He whacks his tail in answer. This could be a scene from a movie – white heat, blue and black girl, smoking bus driver, hot dog. I wish I had my phone to capture this, to own it for ever. She looks up at me, smiles.

'It'll be OK, hun. It will, like,' she says.

I nod and offer her my hand to pull her up. 'Thanks for coming.'

The bus driver flicks his fag away and climbs into the empty bus. Jade hugs me to her, buries her blue head in my chest.

'Love you,' she mumbles.

'Same,' I say, and she peels herself off me and gets on the bus. She waves as the bus pulls away and I'm sad and lonely but glad too, because she can see right inside me.

June

9

I know you're a dream and I pinch myself to wake up but that's part of the dream too, isn't it? You're not like Mam, though – you're a lurker, a shadow player, whispering around on the edges in your football jersey and seaweedy hair and you're dripping, always fucking dripping, and sometimes I hear you, drips like footsteps and I can't see you, just wisps of you and I really want you to fuck off. Mam's enough. And when you're here, she isn't, so just go hang somewhere else …

* * *

I burnt Timber Hanley's halloumi. I was tempted to give it to him anyway, but seeing as he is at present our only regular, I'm frying the halloumi all over again and Timber's whistling at the counter. I know nothing really about Timber. I watch him now as I fry. Leathery face with years of living scribbled on it, like somebody took a pen and dug hard until there were crevices and ravines instead of wrinkles. His hair is a nameless colour, straw-textured with flecks of beige and grey and brown, even flashes of red, like a calico cat. Dad thinks he was a thatcher once until the houses went corrugated or tiled and the drink took hold of him. I make up his wrap and bring it to him, firing on extra salad and lentil crisps. He's sipping his Americano already.

'Powerful shthuff, Saoirse, better than whiskey,' he says as he takes his plate and heads to the window seat. He loves a view of the street with his breakfast. I wipe down the counters again just for something to do. I spend so much time in my own head that I'm now having full-blown conversations with myself. Sometimes I worry that I'm answering myself out loud. I polish the coffee machine – I spend more time with that machine than anyone else. I know it intimately now, its foibles and quirks, how you must coax it in the mornings, how it doesn't like to do too many coffees in a row – that makes it spit and act up, how you must tell it how great it is now and again, like a pet dog.

'Saoirse.'

I jump. Did Joey hear me talking to myself? Fuck.

'Hi, Joey, just giving this machine a rub down ...'

Jesus, you'd swear it was a cow.

'A polish. I'm polishing it.' I smile at him. He looks tired. Did the first lot of bills come in? He's going to sack me. The only thing I have right now is this little job. I need it, both for the money and for my sanity.

'All done with the exams?' He smiles at me, nice white Canadian teeth.

'Yep. We finished on Thursday.'

'How did they go? It must have been so hard after ... you know ... after what happened.'

I polish harder. I want to answer him, to tell him that I loved the exams, the structure, the constant study, the exhaustion at night, the brain wipe-out. I want to tell him about how I managed to avoid Malcolm for the two weeks, with his shiny head and his 'I hear you' face. I want to tell him that I avoided Megan and her friends except for Cian who was sitting in front of me with his sore ear. I want to tell him about Finn. About Finn's empty desk that first day, the slap of reality it gave me, the finality of it.

'They were grand,' I say. 'Easy.'

'That's good. Listen, Melanie came up with a fantastic idea. Music nights. They're big business in Vancouver.'

'That's nice,' I say.

'Friday nights and we can expand if the crowds come and I think they surely will.'

I love Joey's optimism. This is Cloughmore – they go to bingo and set-dancing and the pub. Mass on a Sunday and GAA in season. I can't picture them coming in here for wine and craft beer and lentil curls while listening to Joey sing old songs badly.

'You can play – I heard you playing my guitar. You've such a gorgeous voice. You can MC it too – you know the run of the place – and I'll do chef's specials. I can experiment with the menu. Quinoa burgers, beetroot tarts, that kind of thing.'

I'm hoping this is a Joey fad and won't materialise. 'I ... well ... sounds good,' I say, kicking it to touch.

Joey punches the air. 'I'll get the posters done up. I need a picture of you with your guitar.'

Oh Christ. No. 'Fine. And Joey?' He's already off out the door, full of this new venture.

'Yeah?'

'No veggie burgers. No beetroot. Baskets of chips, onion rings, Manny impersonators, popcorn.'

'That's a great idea, Saoirse, and much cheaper. Sweet potato fries instead of chips?'

'No. Chips. Real chips made from spuds.'

'I got ya.' And he's gone.

'All right, love?' says Timber from his corner. 'Can I have a drop of water for the coffee? 'Tis getting a bit cold and 'tis fierce strong. Even for me and I'd drink petrol.'

I bring him hot water and a slice of organic ethically friendly apple tart and free-range cream.

'You're a great woman. Have you any fella? You've not much to choose from around here. Shower of inbreds.'

'Timber!'

'Sure you're no-one in this town unless you're married to your cousin. I wouldn't like to see their family trees. Fucked up if you ask me. Only place I lived where you're thought more of if you marry your own.'

'You're full of it today, Timber.'

He touches his head. 'Clarity, Saoirse, clarity. I'm on the dry since this morning.'

'That's good, Timber. I hope you stick it out.'

'I will,' he says, looking at the wall clock, a driftwood affair with shells stuck on, 'until five. I'll be going to Custy's then to collect my winnings. Sam's Hero – forty-five to one – got a great tip.'

Timber is even more optimistic than Joey.

*   *   *

Dad's picking me up and Dad and exact times don't mix well. I'm in my nook with my Kindle. This is the one piece of technology I love. I justify that love by where I live. The town library is tiny and if you order a book online, you must answer a million questions when you go to collect it. *Another book on how the brain works? Sure you must know by now after all the others. That book's boring, are you sure you want it?* That's if Mary, the older librarian, is on. If it's Linda, it's a different story. She doesn't make eye contact. She doesn't say hello, goodbye or how can I help you. I don't exist. She's Cian Burke's aunt and Megan's godmother. That's how this town works.

I hear banging. Dad's at the window, knocking like crazy. I'd forgotten I'd locked the door. I collect my stuff, grab the keys and head out into the sunshine.

'Sorry, Dad, I'll just lock up.'

'You were in another world. I was knocking for ages. I'm parked down the road – we're going to Lord's Cove for a coffee with Nana,' he says. 'There's a café there she likes.' He's carrying a box of lettuce. 'Have to drop this into Manny's first.'

Lord's Cove. That's where they hang out. It's their place. I don't want to go, and not with Nana. I march down the street, wondering if I can get out of it. I'm also wondering why Manny needs lettuce and if Timber's horse came in.

* * *

Nana insists on sitting outside Ruby's – the cool place facing the prom and the sea. She's wearing her 'going to the beach for a few days' clothes. Knee-length floral shorts, a bright pink vest and a baseball cap. I love that about Nana – she doesn't give a shit what people think. Eva's sitting opposite her in skin-tight short shorts and a bikini top. Her hair is tied up in a messy bun that took hours to get just right and she doesn't need sun cream. Her full face of make-up suffices. I'm enjoying Eva's discomfort at being landed in full view with her uncool family. I think Nana's enjoying it too. Nana's digging into her carrot cake with a spoon. Aran's buried in his Switch. Dad's stretched out like a cat, eyes closed, taking in the sun.

'Are you delighted to be done with the Leaving Cert, love? Your father told me you flew through it. Knew you would, like – brains to burn you have, you take after me. And after what happened and all. Did you hear my news?'

I shake my head.

'Archie's home. I found him myself.'

Nana leaves a big pause for effect.

'Where was he?'

'Wait until I tell you, Saoirse. He was out in Castleconnell and I was right all along.' Nana's eyes fill up with tears and I'm wondering if she's had a gin already.

'I stalked all them lost and found pages on the Facebook and a woman contacted me yesterday morning. She was feeding a black cat for the past three weeks. So there.' Nana leans back as if she's answered all the questions.

'How did he get there, though?' I say. 'Did he get the bus?'

Aran snorts.

'It was her, yer wan from two doors down,' Nana says, eyes shining at reliving the experience. 'She was seen dropping him off in her Micra – that bitch nun. I swear, I collected Archie and I called straight down to her and told her she was seen – that we'd video evidence – though we haven't, like. I got her good so I did.'

'Poor Archie,' I say.

'No fear of him. He came back with a belly, the whole place was feeding him. And she came over before I left this morning with a green velvet cushion with my Archie's name embroidered on it. The cheek, like? Straight into the bin it went, right there in front of her.' Nana leans back, arms folded across her chest. 'Did you hear me, John?'

No answer from Dad. Eva's examining her dark purple nails. I'm sipping my peppermint tea. The volcano stomach is active today.

'Is his prostrate at him? He's always tired. He should have it checked, that's how his father died, bad prostrate,' Nana says, pointing her spoon at Dad. 'I'm having awful trouble with my sacred iliac – did I tell you that, Saoirse?' She roots in her bag for a cigarette.

I love Nana. She makes everything better. She's paracetamol for the soul.

'How are you, love? How are the bowels after ... you know ... all that business with Finn?'

Here we go with the shit talk. Eva's sniggering into her Coke.

'Grand, Nana. I'm grand.'

'I told you, didn't I, Eva? Didn't I tell your sister? I told you you'd be grand when you got out of that convent. Convents make you mad. They should be banned.'

'I love it there, Nana,' says Eva, smiling at me.

'Ah, sure you love everything,' says Nana, winking at me.

'I can think of a few things I hate,' says Eva, throwing me one of her dead-eye glares. 'I've to go soon, Nana. I'm going to a beach party.' She smiles at Nana, then checks her phone. Bitch.

'Ah, to be your age again. Though 'twas far from beach parties we were reared. We'd be off down in Poorman's Kilkee, a gang of us, delighted with ourselves, with a bottle of Tawny wine – Jesus, that stuff was poison – I can still taste it. Sure ye're all flash now with cocktails and fancy drinks.'

Eva gets up, wiping crumbs from her shorts. She leans towards Nana and hugs her.

'See you later, Nan,' she says.

'You're a good girl, Evie. You've a heart of gold. Hasn't she, Saoirse?'

Eva smiles and picks up her phone and sunglasses.

'Isn't that your friend over there, Saoirse? The skinny one with the witchy face? Finn's sister, isn't she? What's her name again, Maggie? Megan? That's it, Megan.'

They're walking down the prom, the usual bunch. They've spotted us and Megan has a protective circle around her, like I'm Conor McGregor, looking for a fight. Like I'm unhinged. This is new.

'I'll call them over ...'

'No, Nana,' I say, my voice whispery and jerky. My lungs are closing. I can't get air into them. Eva's laughing softly to herself and if my lungs were at full capacity, I'd slap her hard across her orange face.

'Woo hoo, Megan,' Nana says. She's up and out of her seat and I can't follow her to stop her because I can't breathe and my head feels light and my fists are balls of sweat. She's talking to them, chatting to them like they're still my friends, like nothing has happened when a whole world of things has happened.

I hit the floor hard. I think I'm having a heart attack – the pain in my chest is that bad. I can see people's feet. Red Converse, flip flops, Dad's leather sandals, Nana's runners with the diamonds at the side. Somebody's shouting.

I look up and Dylan's there, stroking my hair. There's nobody else there, just Dylan. My lungs fill and I feel so tired. I have to close my eyes, they won't stay open. But I don't want the stroking to stop or Dylan to go away. When I open them again, I can breathe. Dylan is behind me, holding my head. There's a man with a small black dog holding my chin and examining my eyes. Dad and Nana's faces hang over me like weird baubles in too-bright sunlight. I'm raging with myself – stretched out on the prom like some stupid Jane Austen character and Dylan, of all people, tending to me.

'Are you in pain? I'm a doctor,' says the dog owner.

'I ... my chest tightened. I couldn't breathe,' I say. My voice is raggy.

'Do you suffer from panic attacks?' He's staring at my face, probing me with his doctor eyes. I don't want to say it here, in front of the crowd who gathered for a gawk. I nod at the doctor.

'You're fine. Take it easy for the evening. And go see a counsellor, that'll help you deal with the attack. I had panic attacks right through my college years, nothing to worry about. You feel like you're going to die while they're happening, though.' He stands up and chats to Dad and Nana.

Nana takes over. Boxes my life into tight sentences. Black and white. *She's had a tough time what with her mother passing away from cancer and then her ex dying and you know how it is with pals and then that stupid Leaving Cert. I told you, John, she's not happy here. I mean, moving them from a city to the sticks so you could be a pretend farmer. I don't know where you got that notion from. We're good with sums or music. You got those mad ideas from your father's side. You're very good, doctor, isn't he, John? We'll make an appointment with her counsellor ...*

Nan's voice trails on. She's telling everybody my business. I try to spot Megan and the gang but I can't see them. I can hear Aran crying.

I sit up, Dylan helping pull me to my feet.

'Let's get you home,' Dad says.

'I'm not sick,' I say. My legs are shaky. I feel tired and so sweaty. I hate the after-effects of a panic attack more than the attack itself. I hate the way everything in my head seems skewed and filtered. I feel empty. Discombobulated. I love that word for being so accurate.

'You're grand, aren't you, Saoirse?' Nana's holding my hand. 'Did you say thanks to that young man?'

'Thanks,' I say to Dylan's chest.

'Are you all right? I can give you a lift home,' he says. 'It's on my way.'

I shake my head. 'I'm fine. See ya.'

He walks off to join the others.

'Lovely boy,' Nana says.

All the Nana-love feelings are gone. I want to thump her for talking to Megan, for making me anxious, for listing my grievances to all on the prom. At least she didn't bring my dodgy stomach into it.

*   *   *

I play guitar for the evening, losing myself in chords and notes and tunes. I teach myself three new songs and laugh when I realise I'm secretly preparing for Joey's music night. It excites and terrifies me in equal parts and makes me think of Finn and the way he loved my singing. I think that's what attracted him. He attached a whole persona to me that was all in his head. I'd heard that before – that girls fall for guys who play guitar; the reverse is true too. The house is night-quiet, even Aran is in bed. I'm working on a tricky chord sequence when I hear a car pull up and then the front door bangs. Eva. I keep playing, waiting to hear her pound up the stairs. She doesn't. The living room door opens and she comes in.

'Why didn't you answer him?'

She has a hand on her hip as she spits this out. Her make-up is melting and she looks pure frozen in her shorts and bikini. I keep strumming. She edges closer, sits down on the footstool, right in front of me.

'Why didn't you answer him? He called you the night before, and the day he ... the day he died. What kind of cold-hearted bitch are you?'

'My phone was broken – and anyway it's not your business, Eva.' I put the guitar down on the couch beside me and click on the TV, just to fill the space with noise and pictures. She grabs the remote and clicks it back off.

'*My phone was broken* – lamest excuse in the book. Cian's right – you fucked Finn up. And then you wouldn't even take his calls. Do you ever, like, stop looking for notice? It's always about you – Mam dying was all about you, same with moving here – you again, why can't you just fucking be normal?'

'You'll wake the others. Nana's just overhead ...'

'Oh, please – like you care about anyone except yourself? Your carry-on today, even? The big fainting act? Megan's in bits and you don't give one fuck ... Imagine how she felt watching you today? They were all talking about it at the party – about you.'

She's crying, but it's anger tears. She wipes her eyes with the back of her hand, leaving mascara trails on her face.

'What is wrong with you? Why do you want everyone to hate you? A misery guts is what you are – you fucking love being miserable and you love making everyone around you miserable too.'

She stands up, thumps my guitar and marches to the door. I wait for the bang but it doesn't come. She's still here.

'They can read all your messages, your chats with Finn, all of it. You know that, don't you?'

'That's my business, Eva. Nobody else's.'

'So is it true? What they're saying? That you cheated on Finn?'

'No. And again, that's my business. Not yours or Megan's or Cian's. How about believing me for once?'

That produces the door bang. My hands are shaking and sweaty. She stomps upstairs and tries to slam our bedroom door too but she still hasn't learned that it's stiff. My face is slimy with held-in tears. Eva is right. I am a misery guts and I infect anyone close to me.

And I cheated on Finn.

10

Things I didn't know.

Skype and Spotify were founded in Sweden. It's also one of the most successful countries in the world at creating and exporting digital products. And here's the thing – over three and a half thousand Swedes have chips inserted into themselves, grain-of-rice-sized microchips beneath the skin between their thumbs and index fingers. The chips, which cost around a hundred and fifty dollars, can hold personal details, credit-card numbers and medical records. They rely on radio frequency ID, a technology already used in payment cards, tickets and passports. These can be used to pay at vending machines and to log in to computers. Individuals can order do-it-yourself kits, which come with sterilisation tools and a needle to inject the device, or attend 'implant parties', where a professional gives chips to a group. Sometimes they get T-shirts that say 'I got chipped'.

Is this the future? Will we eventually have our phones in a chip under our skin, making our social media 'live' if we so wish? Sometimes I think I should have been born in the stone age, scraping pictures on cave walls.

Other things I didn't know. Tonight is The Bad Seed music night. I'd forgotten and now I'm in a state of anxiety so high I'm hiding in a corner of the café with my Kindle, reading articles about Swedes and relentless technology. I didn't know that Nana left – how did that pass me by? Maybe I have Alzheimer's, some strange form of it that burrows into the brain of teenagers.

Days seem to melt into each other so that time is on a loop. Like when Mam died and I moved into an in-between space where time didn't work any more.

'Saoirse?'

Jesus, Joey, cop on. I hate when people do that right in the middle of a good think.

'I'm here,' I say, uncurling myself from the couch. I love that couch.

'What do you think?'

He's standing at the window admiring his work. He has put red string lights across the glass in brothel fashion.

'Lovely, Joey. Very warm and inviting.'

'I've all the food prepped. I think we'll get a great crowd. I put posters up in Lord's Cove too. All the surfers said they'd come.'

'That's nice,' I say, but I know this place better than Joey. Nobody'll come.

'We'll open at eight. Can you put candles on the tables?'

'Sure.' I begin to work, putting red candles into holders

and arranging sprays of wildflowers in red vases. Joey is obsessed with red.

There are many things I didn't and don't know. Take the Human Brain Project for example. The EU has invested billions into this to create an ICT-based infrastructure for brain research, cognitive neuro-science and brain-inspired computing, which can be used by researchers world-wide. What they're really doing is trying to see if the human mind can be simulated by computer algorithms.

Joey's setting up the mic, and the feedback from the amp's interrupting my mind walks.

Brains are amazing. That's something I do know. They constantly reorganise themselves, both physically and functionally, as a result of actual experience. The brain works on a loop: integration between information and brain matter is ongoing, so the eejits trying to replicate the brain – reduce it to data and algorithms and codes – are on a giant loser. You can't replicate a human. Fuck it, they haven't found a cure for cancer yet, so I rest my case.

And I have a new niggle in my stupid brain. Climate change. Humanity has wiped out sixty per cent of animals since 1970. This is the Moore's Law of wildlife. A world, very soon, without animals. We're all going down the river, literally. Climate change beats technology any day in the worry stakes. My hands are sticky with sweat and my lungs have deflated like popped balloons. I hold on to the table, the wobbly one near the counter, and try to Malcom-breathe. This anxiety is a fucking algorithm. The minute it manifests itself in any form – like, say, performing at a music night in a town where everyone hates you – then all its little soldiers come to bolster it. All the worries, with their spidery arms and legs, weave themselves into the web of your brain. Bastards.

'I made us tea,' says Joey from behind the counter.

He comes around and forces me to sit down at the wobbly table. He sits opposite and places peppermint tea in front of me. I sip it, just to keep him happy.

'You're nervous,' he says. 'That's natural. I'm always nervous when I perform. Surfing's worse for nerves.' He has dressed up for the big night, Levi's, cowboy boots, check shirt. Joey's an old soul in a young man's body.

'How is it worse? Surfing?'

'It's more the thought of it than actually doing it. I surfed Aileen's, the big wave out by the cliffs. That's why we came to Ireland, Melanie and I – to surf her.'

'How do you know she's a girl?'

'Figure of speech.'

'She's probably gender-fluid – all that water.' I laugh at my own stupid joke. Joey smiles but he looks confused. Canadian confused.

'Yeah, the first time we surfed her – it – Melanie chucked up her breakfast. She had a meltdown before we got on the jet skis to ride out.'

'You?'

He grins. 'I do internal anxiety. I hold it all together and then collapse under it eventually.'

'I do both.'

'Thing is, though, it's never as bad once it's started. In fact, it's mostly better than you ever think. I mean, Mel that day, she was something else on that wave, better than all of us. She had her meltdown and got on with it.'

I fiddle with my teacup. I want to be Melanie – a good puke and the anxiety disappears.

'You'll be great tonight, Saoirse. Wait and see.'

'Are we ready to open?' I say.

'You know you can talk to me, right? I was once your age, I know what high school is like. Kinda hell.'

'It's almost eight. I'll open up.'

I walk towards the door, flick the lock and switch the sign.

Timber's in the door before I even finish. ''Tis a wet one out there and we weren't even promised rain. I said it this morning when I saw the cloud over Clare Mountain, I said we'll have rain by night.'

'Hi, Timber.'

'Are you going to throw us a few tunes, love?'

'Yep.'

''Tis only lovely in here. I'll light the candles for ye.'

Joey puts a plate of chips and falafels down on the wobbly table. 'Eat that first, Timber.'

Good old Joey. Except then he goes up to the makeshift stage, an old crate from the timber yard, and launches into an Eagles song. 'Hotel California'. I want to slit my wrists but Timber loves it.

'Hey, love, while he's singing, what are them ball things?'

'They're falafels, Timber. Try them.'

Timber examines the falafels, touches them with his fork until he breaks through the crust.

''Tis very foreign looking. I don't know would I be able for that.'

'Give it a go.'

Joey has moved on to 'Take It Easy'. My dad's party piece. Timber's eating the chips but staring at the falafels like they're alive. He has a quick taste and starts coughing.

'Jaysus, they're little balls of fire, those yokes. He'll be insulted with me now if I don't clear them.'

'I'll dump them for you, you're grand,' I say.

The door clicks open and Dad comes in.

'Dad? What are you doing here?'

'I came to hear you play. I haven't heard you play since ... well, for a while.'

I swallow my knot of anxious and the volcano in my stomach gurgles. Anxiety is fuel for the volcano. Lumps of coal and wood and turf for the smouldering fire in my belly. I go behind the counter and give the coffee machine a quick rub down. It's just Dad. And Timber. Our audience for the night. It's grand. Joey has craft beer chilling in the fridge and I'm tempted but I know that if anxiety is fuel then alcohol is petrol. Dad's chatting to Timber and Joey's moved on to Bruce Springsteen. The door rattles again and the elderly couple who always come in for a pot of tea and ask for bacon and cabbage enter. They shuffle towards the counter.

'A pot of tea, please, and some of those almond slices,' the woman says. 'Do you want an almond slice, Paddy?'

'Have they any apple tart and a bit of cream?' He sits at the table next to Dad.

She gives Timber a glare and nods to her husband to move. He obeys.

'Bingo was cancelled so we saw the lights,' she says.

'I'll bring your tea and cake over. That's eight euro, please.'

She pays me and I want to slap her hard across the face. Instead I smile and busy myself with her tea. Bitch. The bell jangles again and Eva and a bunch of her friends come in, all high heels and high voices. Fuck. One of them, Lisa, I think – but they all look the same – comes to the counter and the others sit as far away from Dad as possible. They are almost sitting in the loo. They sound like Dad's chickens when they see the food bucket.

'Am ... four of those beers, please, the ones with the red label,' she says.

'Sorry, can't serve you alcohol, you're underage,' I say, preparing the tray for the old couple. I smile at her. She has clumps of mascara under her eyes. I know if I see her tomorrow without make-up I won't recognise her.

'I've ID – look,' she says, producing a card from a tiny clutch bag. I glance at the card. It's like something a kid made in art class.

'That's not acceptable. Sorry.' I walk over with the tray and slap it down in front of the elderly couple. The woman is still glaring at Timber, who's slugging from a hip flask. Eva and her friends are whispering and dead-eyeing me. A throng of people arrive then and Joey comes down from the stage to help. I'm paralysed behind the counter. Faces float towards me, Kate, Cian Burke with his wonky ear, Megan at the back, laughing with the Clancy twins. I want to run. Eva's bunch have circumvented the alcohol laws by bringing their own. I can see them slipping flasks to each other. Joey launches into 'Take It Easy'. Again. Timber stands up for this one and Megan and her posse laugh. Cian Burke strolls up to the counter. Kate's beside him, pulling his sleeve. The Clancy twins have their cameras out, filming. There's a symphony of whale noises in my stomach, loud and fiery. I feel hot and sick. Cian says nothing. Stands there, looking at me. Then he smiles. He's wearing vampire teeth.

11

'Stop it, Cian, it's not funny,' says Kate, her voice rising above the laughs and sniggers. 'Stop filming, you bastards.'

Cian is miming a biting frenzy. All I can see are the teeth, huge in his distorted mouth. I grip the edge of the counter, not for support, but to stop me punching him or maybe biting him again.

'I'm sorry, Saoirse, I didn't know anything about this,' Kate says, giving me the big-eyed concerned look. 'Cop on, Cian – just go away.'

Cian winks at me and walks away, followed by the twins.

'Saoirse?' She pats my hand this time. I whip it behind my back.

'Fuck off, Kate. You knew he was going to do it. Just fuck off over to your friends.'

'Is everything OK?' Joey says, appearing behind the counter.

'Fine,' I say. 'Just fine.'

'Good. You're up, Saoirse, they all want chips,' says Joey. 'I knew this was a great idea.'

I make my way to the stage, legs shaky, hands slick with sweat. I pick up my guitar and sit on the high stool. Dad's giving Joey a hand at the counter and he waves at me and gives me a thumbs up. I don't think I can sing. I can't get enough air into me. I strum the guitar and watch my fingers move across the strings. When I look up, more people have spilled through the door. I see him then, at the very back of the room, towering over everyone. He smiles at me and mouths *You got this*. I sing to him, to Dylan, and all the faces fall away and it's just us, in a small café in a small town on the west coast of Ireland. I sing songs I had never dared to sing in public before – a mash up of 'No Diggity' and Britney, followed by Bruce Springsteen and good old Bon Iver's 'Skinny Love'. I put the guitar down, still looking at Dylan. People start to clap, some even stand up. I walk towards the counter and Dylan grabs my arm.

'That was great, Saoirse. I always loved your voice but that was something special. I heard what Cian did – ignore him, he's just –'

'He's just your pal,' I say.

We've run out of beer and Joey's all set to beg some from the nearest pub when he gets the call. Melanie's in labour. I urge him out the door, telling him not to worry and to drive safely. But there's no driving – of course there isn't – it's a home birth. I start the wash-up as the crowd take turns singing. One of Eva's friends has a gorgeous voice and a lovely strum on guitar. I stop to listen to her for a minute and her voice carries through the room, silencing even the drunks. Dad has left. He is rigorous about bedtime. I check the clock. Another hour max and I'll be home. I check the till and can't get over the novelty of its fullness. I'm happy for Joey but I don't know how I'll face this again. Just seeing them all laughing, enjoying themselves, makes me feel shit about myself, like I don't deserve friends. Worthless.

Timber wanders up to the mic before I can stop him and starts singing a *sean nós* song. It's lovely, if he wasn't langers and slurring his words in between forgetting them. The song has about a million verses and he stops suddenly, looks at all of us and cries. He continues to sing, tears running down his face. One of the twins takes out his phone and starts recording him, to a soundtrack of laughing and sniggering. Eva, the fool, is sitting on Cian's lap. My volcano stomach erupts and I have this black urge to hurt – no – to kill. Not any particular one – all of them, every one of them with their sneery, judgey heads.

Timber launches into yet another verse and combines the crying with the song this time. It's kind of heart-breaking, but my ex-friends think it's hilarious. Cian's recording it too and egging poor Timber on. I march over, grab his phone and fling it against the wall. The clock drops to the floor. I turn to the twins, manage to grab another phone from them and throw it. It doesn't hit the wall, lands instead in a vase of flowers on a shelf, tumbling to the floor in a pool of phone, water and wildflowers. The place is silent: even Timber has stopped the cry-singing.

'Get out. You, Cian Burke, and those two gowls – out. Now.' My voice is calm.

Cian stands up, looks at his smashed phone. 'You'll pay for this, you fucking crazy bitch. That's a brand-new phone.'

'Get out,' I say.

His eyes bulge as he lunges towards me. Dylan rugby-tackles him to the ground and there's screaming and Dylan is sitting on Cian, punching him.

'Dylan,' I say, pulling his arm, 'stop it. Stop now.'

Dylan rolls off Cian. He stands up, wiping his forehead. Timber launches into another verse like nothing happened. Cian gets up, dusts himself down and pushes past Eva. He eyeballs me and turns his back, walking towards the door. He picks up the wobbly table, knocking candles and drinks to the floor and lugs it at the window. The table leg catches in the netting on the ceiling, bringing it down on top of people. More screaming. It's a cartoon image – as people try to free themselves, the netting becomes fierce, wrapping itself around arms and legs and heads. I laugh at the chaos and incongruity. To top it off, Timber starts another verse from the song that keeps on giving. I try to undo the knot of net and bodies.

'Why did you do that?' says Eva, as she marches to the door with her posse. 'You need help.'

'Yep – netting is a fucker to untangle,' I say.

'Fucking drama queen – can't take a bit of fun. Ever,' she says. 'You're a mess – that's why everyone hates you.' She elbows her way past me.

The café empties in a dream. Faces float in front of me but it's like I've detached myself from it all. Megan lowers her eyes as she leaves, afraid to look at me in case she turns to stone. I'm holding the broken clock and I have to pinch myself so that I don't throw it at her head. Timber's asleep in the cosy nook. I survey the damage – the damage that I can see. I walk to the storeroom to get sweeping brushes and the mop, and I scream when I see Dylan coming out of the loo.

'Jesus, sorry, Saoirse ... I ... I'll give you a hand with this mess.'

'No need. The door is that way,' I say, grabbing brushes and mops. He follows me out to the café and takes a brush and pan. I pick up the net and roll it into a ball. We work together in silence, sweeping up broken phones and glass and debris. Dylan loads the dishwasher and wipes down the tables. He finds a ladder in the store and fixes the netting back up on the ceiling.

'There,' he says. 'You'd hardly know the difference.'

'Thanks,' I say. 'I'd offer you a beer but they drank us dry.'

'A coffee'd be great,' he says, sitting down at a table. 'What'll we do with Timber?'

I crank up the coffee machine. It purrs into life straight away, like it's thrilled to be of use. I pat it as it does its thing.

'We'll wake him up when we're leaving.' I make two espressos, though I know it'll kill my stomach and my sleep, but I think sleep tonight is not happening anyway. I bring the cups to the table. I can hear Timber snoring in the corner.

'Cian's a dick,' says Dylan and sips his coffee. The tiny cup looks silly in his hand. 'He's ... he's just ... brainless.'

I want to go home. I want to be in my bedroom, safe and alone. I want to never leave that room again. I slug back my coffee.

'Look – they're ... I don't know ... immature, I suppose. And we're all fucked up after Finn. I kept waiting for him to walk in here tonight – big smile, calming the eejits down. I miss him, Saoirse.'

He rubs his face with his hands. When he looks up, he's crying. Proper fat tears that he doesn't wipe away. And then I'm at it too, head down, crying into my chest, giving our Aran a run for his money.

'I miss him too. It's like the exams helped me not to think about him – you know – about it all and now ... now I ...'

I manage to stop myself before I tell Dylan that Finn's invading my dreams, along with my dead mother. He leans forward, half hugs me, rubs my hair. I lift my face to his and we're kissing, hands all over each other and it's what I want but it's weird and Dylan's drunk and Timber's snoring in the corner. I pull away.

'I'm sorry,' he says. 'I didn't mean to ... you know ...'

'It's fine. I didn't either. It's just that ... I haven't been able to miss him properly, like – in our group of friends – or ex-friends.'

'I know. They're all hurting and looking for one thing to blame – or one person. It doesn't work like that.'

'He called me. That night and the next morning. He fucking called me and I'd busted my phone off a wall and ...' The tears come again in a snotty gush.

'Did he leave a message?'

I shake my head. 'The phone is in bits in my drawer. I can't listen, I can't.'

'It might help, but take your time, Saoirse. We're all fucked up. My mam's driving me crazy – she's, like, hovering all the time, watching me in case I do it. And Dad's just a typical old man – talking to me about football and college and the dog down the road who's worrying his sheep. And that's easier – do you know what I mean?'

'Yep. Like my granny. And Jade. My dad's a hoverer as well. I wonder if they have some sort of WhatsApp hovering group going?'

'Mine'd sign up for that. They've been hovering since I was born. Only child syndrome.'

'I keep forgetting that. You can have our Eva if you want. I'll throw in Aran too.'

He laughs. 'Sometimes I think that ... you know ... that we're all having tiny little breakdowns all the time and sometimes they all add up into a giant one and maybe that's what happened to Finn? He never said anything to me, though – always so happy – fucking dumb word – happy. I'm drunk, aren't I?'

'*In vino veritas.*'

'What's that? Anyway, yeah – I told him stuff – when I was feeling like crap and he was so fucking together and cool about it and then ... this shit.'

'Finn didn't have all the answers, Dylan. Sometimes he'd tell you what you wanted to hear, even if that meant lying.'

'What do you mean?'

I shrug. 'Just stuff.'

'Jesus. I didn't mean to be nosy, like. I fucking miss him, though. He *lived* in our house. I'm there at night, playing Xbox and, I swear, I forget he's dead and I turn around to slag him or ... like, his name pops up on my screen as highest scorer. It kills me.'

I lean into him and we hug and I want to kiss him but I don't.

'My dad is right, though, Saoirse. Stick to the routine. Plan things. Do normal stuff. He calls it "keeping on". I wasn't going to lifeguard in Lord's Cove this summer – it just felt wrong without Finn. You know, we'd applied together, done the courses together. Anyway, Dad talked me into it. He's a great man for routines. And work.'

'He's right. This job here keeps me sane. Although tonight was a mess ...'

Dylan shakes his head. 'You were brilliant, Saoirse, and that took guts. I really admire you. I wasn't going to come but I'm so glad I did – Dad made me – and when I heard you singing, it reminded me of Finn, but in a good way. Why do I talk so much when I'm pissed? Mam's booked a holiday and I have to go with her cos, like, Dad has the farm as his excuse and apparently the sun will do me good and it doesn't here so why will it in Puerto fucking Banus and, fuck it, I'm tired of the hovering and the fucking expectation, do you know what I mean?'

I shake my head. 'Not really.'

'It's an only-child thing I guess but I'm expected to do things – to go to agricultural college and –'

'What?' I'm laughing at the idea of Dylan at agricultural college. He hates the farm, cows, slurry, silage.

'Yep – Dad thinks I'll be taking over the farm and I haven't the heart to tell them what I really want.'

'Which is?'

'Don't laugh. Promise?'

'Promise.'

'Art college.'

'Seriously?'

'Yep. I submitted my portfolio. Just to see, you know, if I can do it. Ms Collins helped me. Lots of cow sketches – and a beaut of Finn playing the Xbox – you know that mad concentrated face he has ... had.'

'Go for it, Dyl. Go for art college. Limerick?'

'Yep. I mightn't get it, and anyway the parents'll throw a fit. It was Finn who made me apply. He organised my portfolio with me – had checklists and all. Gas man.'

'They'll get over it.'

He leans his head on my shoulder and I run my hands through his hair. I still think he gets free highlights from his mother. I'm thinking of Finn and his checklists. His probability scores, his betting spreadsheets. That was before the gambling really dug its claws into him. That was when he thought he controlled it and not the other way round.

'Dylan, you knew about his gambling, right?'

He lifts his head, my fingers still knotted in his hair. 'Finn? He threw a bet like the rest of us – he was great on odds, all the maths done – I wouldn't call it gambling, exactly. Just a bit of fun.'

And there it is. You can't diss a dead lad. I shouldn't have said anything. I lean into him this time and he pulls my face towards his.

'Where the fuck am I?' says Timber from his makeshift bed. 'Is it a lock-in?'

Dylan's shaking from laughing and it's contagious.

12

I'm reading an article on my break about sadness. How scientists believe they may have caught a glimpse of what sadness looks like in the brain. It was a pitifully small study, conducted in the University of California. Sadness and other emotions involve the amygdala, an almond-shaped mass found in each side of the brain. Even sadness has a house. And there also was evidence that the hippocampus, which is associated with memory, can play a role in emotion. Did it take scientists to work that one out? If we had no memory, then we'd all be grand. They wanted to study what exactly happens when somebody's down, what parts of the brain are engaged. You can't track this stuff on a brain scan because you can't map the changes that occur in fractions of a second.

The door jingles and Joey and Melanie come in, all Canadian sunshine and positivity, new baby strapped to his mother. Avery Carlton Jameson the Third. That's some name to be living up to. He's cute, though, in that baldy, gummy, wrinkly baby way. Melanie is Mother Earth, all giant boobs and folds of Madonna flesh and smiles for everyone. She looks like she's stoned on motherhood. Timber's in my cosy nook, having his now customary free dinner from Joey. Quinoa and beetroot salad today. We've really messed with Timber's palate. I don't know if he could still down a portion of Manny's battered sausage and chips. Joey's started talking to Timber about co-parenting and bed sharing. Timber's eyes have glazed over and it's not from the delights of the quinoa. Melanie's perched at the counter, baby swaddled in some ethically sourced flowery wrap thing that looks complicated.

'I'll be back surfing next week, Saoirse. That's my goal,' she says as she sips Joey's new invention. Matcha coffee. Timber's not a fan. He calls it Shrek's piss.

'That soon?' I continue doing my favourite job, cleaning down the coffee machine.

'Sure. I know lots of surfers who go back, like, straight after the birth. It's no big deal.'

I found a new cloth, a nano-microfibre yoke, and it gets such a shine on the machine. That makes me calm. A shiny coffee machine.

'I can't wait to get back out. It's an addiction. It really is. Hey, Saoirse – did I just hear Joey tell Timber all about the placenta?'

'Yep.' There's a tiny stain on the side of the machine that I can't budge. I think it might be a dent, a little mark from the music night.

'Are you OK?'

I can feel Melanie's eyes on me when she says this but I scrub away.

'I can always feel sadness – you know?' she says.

Definitely a dent. Will not budge.

'I was sad too for a long time. Back in Vancouver. I was about your age – something happened one night, something bad. I pretended it didn't happen. I drank, self-medicated. Counselling saved me. You're still going to counselling, right?'

I bend down to clean the bottom of the machine and Malcolm-breathe to control myself. If Melanie knew anything about sadness, she'd know that telling a sadder story, or her own sad story, won't make a sad person feel better. She'd know that.

'I'm sorry, Saoirse. I get it. I'm being all invasive and silly. I'm sorry.'

There are crumbs on the floor in little clumps, right behind the shelving. I'll have to clean that up or we'll get mice. I stand up and Melanie has moved over to Joey. They're kissing and cooing and Timber's mopping up his dinner with sourdough bread. Dylan and I are meeting for a drink. He texted and I said yes and now I regret it. It feels off. Wrong. I continue to tidy up. I feel tired despite the quiet day here. I've been tired since music night. I get the hoover and suck up all the crumbs behind the counter. There's a whole heap of them, a little feast for vegetarian rodents.

'We're off, Saoirse. Lock up early – you look like you've plans. Have a good one!' says Joey.

They leave and Timber follows, heading straight to Custy's for the six o'clock horse race. Finn taught me well. I must have overdone it with the black dress if Joey noticed. What if I'm overdressed, though? What if Dylan thinks I like him? I should have worn sweats. I make a peppermint tea and sit in the nook. He's late. It's gone six. He's not coming at this stage. I glance out the window, up and down the street. No sign. I wipe down the tables for a second time. Bastard. But in a way I'm relieved. I can go home. To bed. I grab my bag and the bunch of keys and slam the door so hard on the way out the broken clock falls to the floor. I lock the door, fumbling to find the right key. Then I run, race up the street, pushing people out of my way.

'Saoirse? Saoirse, wait up,' a voice calls. I break into a full-on sprint. I can hear feet pounding the footpath and then heavy breathing in my ear. A hand reaches from behind and pulls me to a stop.

'Stop, for fuck sake, stop running,' Dylan says in a scratchy out-of-breath voice.

His face has gone a light pink and the colour is moving down his chin and neck.

'I thought I had the car but Mam had taken it, so I had to run all the way in. She's doing some yoga shit or something and I thought you'd forgotten and the café was locked and ...'

He leans against the wall, still struggling for breath. 'Jesus. I texted your brick phone.'

'I forgot to charge it. Come on, so,' I say. 'Food or pub?'

We end up in Daffy's – Timber's local. Although all the bars in Cloughmore are Timber's local. There's no chance of meeting that other shower in here. It's old style, a narrow corridor of a bar with a tiny snug at the back. There are three regulars at the counter and they look like their arses have been welded there for at least a decade. We head to the cubby hole in the back.

'What are you having?'

He looks at me, afraid to give a wrong answer. 'A pint of Heineken. Here, let me get it.'

'Why? Because you're the man?'

I march up to the bar and call out the order to the sleepy crossword-busy barwoman. The three regulars eye me up without missing a beat in their conversation. Three Cloughmore lads for sure. I take the two pints and bring them back to the table. I'll pay for this in volcanic eruptions but I don't care. I need it for the nerves. So does Dylan, because he gulps down half the pint in one slug.

'You're thirsty,' I say, sipping mine. It tastes like piss.

'I ran three miles in, like, six minutes,' he says.

'Bit of an exaggeration there, I'd say.'

He smiles. 'Sorry I was late. Really sorry.'

I shrug.

'Mam just fecked off in the car and Dad was gone and –'

'I know. You told me already.'

He wipes his palms on his knees. 'I'm sorry ...'

'You told me that too. Twice.'

He picks up his pint and I notice that his hand is shaking. He spills a little onto the table. It drips down on the ancient tiled floor. A tiny shaft of light from a grimy window has found its way into the dark recesses of the pub. There are dancing dust mites around Dylan's head. He's staring at the dripping beer.

'Sorry,' he says to his pint. 'Sorry.'

'Yep. I know.'

He looks at me, the first real eye contact he's made. He has a pimple over his upper lip and I try not to stare at it. I can hear the hum of the conversation in the bar, easy and familiar.

'It's just ... I ... It's just ...' He takes a gulp of beer. 'I'm trying to say ... it's ...' He runs his hand through his hair and shakes his head.

'Are you breaking up with me?' I cackle at my own joke. It was meant to be a soft laugh but it echoes around the almost silent pub.

'Can you just stop, for once?' he says. 'Can you just listen?'

'I'm all ears.' I'm not really. I'm a ball of awkward anxiety. My stomach's bubbling and I want to be at home with Dad and the egg boxes. Anywhere except here.

'I like you.'

'I like me too,' I say. That's a lie but lies are handy for protection.

'Saoirse. Please.'

'I'm sorry,' I say and launch into my new-found cackle.

Dylan smiles. Finishes his beer. 'I know it's weird, like, after Finn and all – I get that ...' He looks at me, knee touching mine. 'I'm sorry, Saoirse, me and my stupid mouth. It's way too weird and soon and fucked up. I'm a gowl, aren't I? Same again?'

'No. Tastes like piss.'

He goes to the bar and I want to slap myself hard. Thump myself into the head with a closed fist. Bite my own ear off. He's chatting at the bar and he looks so comfortable. Pure local. One of the old guys even has an arm around his shoulder. The shaft of light has followed him, making him young and golden and easy in himself. I'm the black mess in the corner, head full of catastrophe and self-pity, stomach spitting acid, brain on fire. He likes me? Why say it now and why did we do everything backwards? He returns with two pints of Guinness.

'Try this, Saoirse. I promise you it's not piss.' He also brings peanuts and a deck of cards. 'Poker,' he says, 'for peanuts. And a promise.'

'Sounds serious.'

He laughs. 'Nope. The debs dance, celebrating end of school, you know?'

'Not going. Are you?'

'Only if you'll come with me.'

Dylan knows how to make the weird weirder.

I shake my head. 'I don't think so – it'd be strange now – you know – with Megan and the others and ...'

'That's just it, though. It's like my dad says, we keep going, we do all the things. Finn would have wanted that – man. He was looking forward to the debs – the rite of passage stuff, you know?'

'And then I finished with him.'

'Jesus, I didn't mean it like that, Saoirse.'

A quiet settles around us and even the locals stop their chatter. The TV in the corner beams silent news to nobody. Horse-racing results. I wonder if Timber's horse came in.

'I think Megan was going to ask you,' I say. 'To the debs, I mean.'

He looks at me and shrugs. 'Now that'd be really weird. And fucking awkward. We went out for, like, two minutes and we had nothing to say to each other except talk about Finn.'

Lads. They really are a different breed. Megan has invoked secret girl-rules around Dylan: he's untouchable even though he doesn't know or care.

He grins. 'Think about it. It'll be good. For all of us. How's your poker face?'

✳   ✳   ✳

He's in the loo and I'm trying to stop my brain from analysing and assessing. *Things I know. It's late. I'm really good at poker. Who'd have thought that? Dylan is sound. I like him. Jade is right. Stop fucking obsessing about everything. Guinness doesn't make my stomach explode. It's been a good night. Even a great one. I'm a bit pissed and it's hilarious. They've locked the door of the pub and the shaft of light has been replaced by bare bulbs. The three locals are still welded to their high stools. They've grown on me a bit. The bar is a haven. A bubble of comfort in Cloughmore. Timber has excellent taste in pubs. I ate my winnings and I have a bucket of peanuts in my stomach. And poker dates are the best.*

He comes back from the toilet and slides in beside me. I can feel the heat off him, thigh pressed to thigh and the peanuts do a somersault. I promise myself that when I get him outside, I'll shift the face off him.

'Tell me more,' he says, touching my hand with his. I hope he can't feel the want off me.

'About what?'

'The mad stuff you're into. The brain stuff.'

'OK. Brains react to alcohol in different ways. Mine clogs up – like a computer with a fog virus. How's that?'

He laughs. 'Same. Now give me something real.'

'The frontal cortex of your brain expanded through evolution and this helped us create language and science.'

'OK. More.'

I sift through my Guinness-fogged head. 'We only use ten per cent of our brain.'

'I read that somewhere. Weird.'

'You read that somewhere and it's a myth. A lie. Ninety per cent of your brain isn't useless filler. Magnetic resonance imaging shows that most of the human brain is active most of the time.'

'You're sexy when you talk about brains.'

He reaches out and touches my face. I feel light-headed, a mixture of alcohol and attraction. Dangerous. And I'd love to pop the pimple above his lip.

'A recent study – I think it was 2013, so not *that* recent – found that sixty-five per cent of Americans believe the myth. No surprise there.'

'You're not a flat-earth fan so?'

I pull away from him. 'Are you? If you are then you're dead to me.'

He grins. 'Nope. My mother'd kill me.'

We both crack up at this. Drunk-laughing and causing the locals to halt their chats. They're watching us from the bar like we're the TV. I lean into Dylan. 'Want to give them something better to watch?'

I'm inches from his face. I kiss him then, full-on shift, and I don't want to stop but pull away before he thinks I'm going to eat him or – worse – bite off his ear.

'Let's go,' he says.

I nod and grab my cardigan. When I stand up. I'm raining peanuts.

'Tell your father I was asking for him,' one of the old guys says to Dylan as we head for the door.

'Will do, Chilli,' Dylan says.

I snigger.

'Is that the egg man's daughter?' says Chilli.

'Are you the egg man's daughter?' says Dylan.

He's laughing and I'm afraid we'll crack up again.

'Yes,' I say to Chilli. 'My claim to fame.' Chilli's eyes are rheumy blue.

'Are you the young wan working in the quare place across the road? Timber's friend?'

'That's me. My other claim to fame.'

Outside, the town is empty. Orange streetlights throw an eerie sodium glow over shopfronts and houses. I'm a bit unsteady on my feet and Dylan isn't much better.

'I like Guinness,' I say.

The full moon is high over the town, adding to the surreal night. A dog barks somewhere, deep and loud and persistent.

'Really?' he says, stopping and leaning against Cod U Not, the now closed alternative chipper to Manny's and favourite of the town rats. Hence the closure.

'Yep.'

He pulls me towards him and we're kissing again, against the blocked-up façade. He tastes of Guinness, salt and more. He tastes of more.

'Chips?' He's looking down into my face.

'Yes,' I say, my voice cracking like he's just asked me to marry him.

'Great.' He launches into another kissing session and the chips are forgotten for at least five minutes.

We're heading towards Manny's again and my woozy brain's recording brand-new images and experiences. I'm walking through Cloughmore, holding hands with a guy I like. He's even from here, this place I hate so much. I've a belly full of Guinness and the volcano has remained dormant. I'm starving and excited and happy. Christ. I'm happy.

'Chilli, though?' I say as Dylan pushes the door of the chipper open with his shoulder.

Manny beams when he sees us. A look-at-you-with-a-fella beam.

'My favourite girl in Cloughmore,' he says. 'And my favourite boy. This is *perfetto*! So, what will I prepare for you?'

Manny talks as if he's running a Michelin-star restaurant.

'I'll have the usual, Manny. Dylan? What do you want?'

He kisses me. 'You.'

'Cheesy gowl,' I say.

'Is that on the menu? Definitely having that. Am ... I'll have the same as her, Manny.'

'Two large chips with cheese coming up,' he says.

'Answer me.' I'm still holding his hand.

'What?'

'Chilli. Why Chilli?'

He smiles. 'His father was Con Kearney – from over the road from me – few fields down.'

'You're such a bogger. A few fields down.'

He shrugs. The door pushes open and it's them, voices high and loud, the smell of perfume and Lynx overpowering the frying chips. They fall silent when they see us. Megan stares at me. I try to hold her gaze. She wins the eye wrestle. I turn my head to the notice board and pull my hand from Dylan's. They swarm up to the counter and I edge away. They're making small talk with Dylan. I fix my eyes on a poster. Misty the cat who's missing since yesterday. She has only one eye. Misty is scared of cars and people and dogs.

Misty's owner is Amanda, aged ten, and she can't sleep at night without Misty.

Misty is wearing a pink collar and she's from Arragh but could have been trapped in a car engine. That's weird about Misty because she hates cars so why would she climb into the engine of one? I move on to the next poster. Are all the animals in Cloughmore on the run?

Dog this time. Nama – missing from Circular Road. Collie cross. Dylan's behind me, I can feel his breath on my shoulder. He places his arms around my waist, in a backward hug. I'm mortified and don't reciprocate but Dylan's playing to the crowd.

'Fuck them,' he whispers in my ear.

'Chips for the lovely couple,' says Manny, for once not picking up on the charged, awkward atmosphere. Dylan goes to pay and takes my hand as we leave. I can feel eyes boring into the back of my skull. I feel at ease. Safe. Dylan's like armour. No vampire noises, no ear-biting jokes.

'Will you do something with me?' I say, digging into the food.

'Love to,' he says. I punch him in the arm and he loses a few chips.

'Can we climb up to the graveyard? I love the view but I'm too scared to go up at night?'

'Come on so, first up to the graveyard gets ... a skeleton.'

He runs off and I follow, panting, after him. Once we head up the hill, only the moon throws light on the old, uneven path. There's an old stone seat almost at the top and Dylan flops down on it. I join him and we finish our chips with Cloughmore spread out in front of us. I can make out Lord's Cove with its string of lights along the prom. I imagine I can hear the sea but it's probably traffic.

'Kiss me,' he says, balling his chip bag and throwing it on the ground. I think of Finn and his obsession with litter.

'No. Not unless you pick that up.'

He laughs, bends down and picks up the bag, pushing it into the pocket of my cardigan.

'Thanks. Just what I wanted.'

'Kiss me.'

I lean over and kiss him. He doesn't move, lets me do all the work. It's nice work. I explore his face with my tongue, my lips. He responds, gentle and slow. Where did he learn how to do that? I push him down on the seat and we kiss and explore some more. I straddle him and try to pull off his T-shirt, my hands rummaging under it first for bare flesh.

'Move, Jesus,' he screams, almost pushing me off him. He gets up and hops around the laneway on one leg.

'I'm sorry ... I ...'

'Cramp. My fucking leg is cramping.'

I laugh, quiet at first but then it takes hold of me. It's the hopping motion and the pained look on his face. He sits back down, rubbing his calf.

'Jesus, that was like being caught in a vice. Sorry, Saoirse.'

I'm still laughing. He joins in.

'It was so ... romantic,' I say.

'Totally.'

I catch his face in my hands and kiss him hard. I'm shocked at myself. At my brazenness. It must be the Guinness. Or the Dylan armour.

'Let's go,' he says.

We walk down the hill in the silver light. He's swinging my hand as he walks, talking away, but I can't hear him. I'm too aware of how good I feel. We're just at the cross when we hear it – a kind of howling – and I look back at the graveyard, high on the hill with the full moon guarding it. I feel cold and I can sense tension in Dylan's hand. Somebody screams, female, followed by shouting.

'Come on,' says Dylan, leaving go of my hand and breaking into a sprint. We follow the sounds like GPS and turn the corner and head towards the river. Cian's standing on the bridge and I can't tell if he's laughing or crying or both as Megan and Kate try to grab his legs. And then he's gone.

13

Dylan's the first to react. I'm a statue on the bridge watching the angry river suck Cian down. I'm shaking and Megan's screaming – or is it Kate? – and I need to do something, anything, so I run down to the riverbank, stinging my legs on the nettles, and the burn wakes me up. The blistering pain clears my fog. Dylan's in the river, slicing through the black water and I take out my phone. My fucking dead phone. Megan's hanging over the bridge but she has her hands over her face and all I see in the water are Cian's white flailing arms and Dylan reaching for him, missing, reaching again and then yanking his dead weight and pulling and yanking and inching him towards the shore.

Dylan has Cian in the recovery position and I'm getting Finn flashbacks and then there's the magic sound of Cian coughing and puking up water. Dylan's lying on his back, looking up at the navy sky. Megan runs to him, hugs him, kisses his mouth and in that moment I want to push her into the black roaring river, boot her in and let her float off down to the sea. Cian sits up, rivulets of water running down his face.

'Fuck, man. I fell, like. I was only messing,' he says. 'Hahaha, that was some laugh, Meg, you lost your shit.'

Megan shakes her head at Dylan.

'You were in trouble there, lad,' says Dylan.

'I was just having a laugh – freaking the girls out. Where's my snack box? Is it still on the bridge?'

There's a nervous ripple of laughter from the others and then they're doing a football huddle, the three of them, but on their knees. I break into a run. I can hear Dylan shouting my name. I run harder.

*   *   *

I can feel what you feel. The water filling your lungs, stealing your air, choking you. You can see the ocean floor, shadowed with rocks and seaweed until the water squeezes your eyes shut. There's pain too, isn't there? If I sit here, on this step, will you show yourself? Talk to me? Why are you always half here? Mam was fully here, she talked to me. You're a cartoon ghost. A lurker. There's no point to you. Mam was comfort. You haunt me. You're a coward.

*   *   *

'Saoirse, wake up.'

Somebody's shaking my shoulder. I slap them away. I don't want to wake up. I want to stay asleep for ever.

'Come on, let's get you to bed.'

'Go away.'

'Bed.'

'I'm tired. I'm grand here.'

I feel myself being lifted and carried. I look up into Dad's face and I feel like a kid again, when I thought Dad was huge and safe and armour. He's not armour. He's a small, broken man. The silence surrounds us. Hugs us. I can hear the birds waking up, lone chirps strengthening to a chorus. The trees in the garden whisper and light breaks in the far field. There's a long sliver, widening all the time.

'Dylan called me. He told me what happened.'

The silver line on the horizon has stretched into the indigo sky. My hands are stiff and sore and ice cold. I furl and unfurl my fists to warm them up.

'It's like what you said, Dad. The copycat thing.'

'Dylan said Cian was messing.'

'Yeah. Sure.'

We're inside the house now, and he lays me on the couch and covers me with a blue throw. Mam's throw.

'It's my fault. I started it. I made Finn sad.' My voice is low and calm. Why am I so calm?

'Sometimes, when we're angry or upset, we blame ourselves for things we have no control over. I do it all the time, Saoirse.'

He reaches out and touches me and I bury my head in a mixture of throw and Dad.

'It'll be OK – all of it. You'll see. You're not responsible for the world.'

'If Dylan hadn't been there, I mean the current was crazy and ... I thought he was dead too. Lungs full of water, like Finn. It's dominoes, Dad, and I'm the first domino to fall. You said it yourself, it's contagious. I'm contagious.'

'Ah stop, Saoirse.'

'No. It's true. It is. Cian jumped. I was there. And now we're all pretending he was messing.'

'I found you on the doorstep. Asleep. Why didn't you come in, love?'

I rub my eyes, and poor Dad thinks I'm crying. I'm not. I'm trying to remember blacking out. For hours. I can't. It's like the hard drive in my brain has been wiped. I know the after-effects. I can feel it in my body.

The door opens and Aran comes in, eyes round and wet.

'Did somebody die?' he says.

'No, Aran. There was a bit of an accident in town, that's all,' says Dad.

'I heard Saoirse. He didn't fall,' says Aran. 'He tried to do it too.'

He full-on cries now and I pull him towards me and the snots come, strings of them on Mam's throw.

'Can I stay here with you? Can I?'

'If you want. There's no room on the couch, though.'

'I'll sort it,' says Dad.

He leaves, and Aran's cries have eased to sniffles. Aran doesn't move, he's welded to me and my eyes are dropping. Blackouts exhaust me. If that's what they are. Dad arrives back with cushions and duvets and makes a nest for Aran on the floor. Aran crawls into it, tugging it close to the couch. Dad heads to bed, switching off lights as he goes.

'Saoirse.'

'Mmm?' I'm too tired to form words.

'I miss Mam.'

'So do I. Go to sleep, Ar, it's late.'

'I miss her smell.'

'Mmm.'

'And her lasagne. Dad's is all watery.'

'Yep.'

'I don't want to go to secondary school. It's too scary.'

'It'll be grand.'

'It won't. I'm not like Eva, I'm like you. It'll be horrible. I've heard stories.'

'There's always stories. You'll like it.'

'No, I won't. I'll have to pretend – like you do. I miss my pals back home. In Limerick. They don't like me here. They say I'm weird and a whinger. Do you like it here?'

'I like the farm and the chickens and Izzy Goat. You couldn't have those in Limerick.'

'That's stupid, Saoirse. If we hadn't moved, then I wouldn't have met them. Gowl.'

'Go to sleep.'

'If you liked here, then so would I cos we're the same.'

'I'm tired, Ar.'

'I miss Finn too. He was so funny. We had farting competitions and we named our farts and we even recorded them. Do you want to listen?'

I pretend I'm asleep but I've a pain in my throat from swallowing the urge to cry.

'You won't do it, Saoirse, sure you won't?'

'Do what?'

'What Finn did. You won't do that on me.'

I can't answer. The tears have come.

*   *   *

Malcolm has had the waiting room painted. It's a soft yellow, the colour of scrambled eggs. I can still get the whiff of fresh paint despite the candles dotting the room. I have nothing to say to Malcolm, but Dad insisted I go and he needs to believe I'm OK. I can smell the worry off him. And we had to wait a few days for an appointment. Malcolm's making a fortune out of all of this.

'Saoirse. Come in,' says Malcolm from the door of his office. I follow him, glad and disappointed that I can hear him. The glugging came back after the Cian incident. The 'messing' incident.

'How are you?'

I shrug. I don't know if I'll make it through a whole hour of this. And anyway, how the fuck does he think I am?

'It's a process. Grieving. Be kind to yourself, Saoirse. You've dealt with so much over the last few years.'

Be kind to myself. Tea-towel phrases. He should put all his little self-help gems on mugs and keyrings and tea towels. A little sideline for when the world realises he's a big fraud. I'd be better off talking to the chickens or the goat.

'Are you still taking your anti-depressants?'

'Yep.'

'That's good.'

I can see him examining my face for lies.

'They help a little,' I say, throwing him a bone. The truth is I took them for a few days months ago and they gave me electric shocks in my brain and made me feel sick. I stashed them, filled the prescription every month and lied. I also researched them and that scared me.

'Good, good, good. How are things at home?'

Another shrug from me.

'Work?'

Shrug.

'Social life? Are you doing anything that gives you pleasure?'

'Not at the moment,' I say. I smile at him. Another bone. He needs it. He laughs too loud at my weak joke.

'Work? Are you coping with work?'

'Yes.'

Malcolm's staring at me. I can feel his eyes boring into my head, digging and prying. I know what my job is: I must make Malcolm believe that I'm managing. I'm enjoying this silence, though. Two can play the silence game.

'Let's talk about Finn. Have you had any closure?'

I pick my fingers under the desk. The candle nearest me fizzles and dies.

'Come on, Saoirse. You can talk here. This is a safe place.'

'There's nothing to talk about. He died.'

'How did it make you feel?'

I glare at him. I'd love to punch him into the mouth. A solid thump to make him stop talking.

'How do you think it made me feel?' My voice is a whisper. I wanted to shout it at him but this tiny sound comes out instead.

'Sad. Angry. Guilty. All normal, all OK. I heard about the incident the other night. How did that make you feel?'

'Like it's contagious. Like something started with Finn and it's running through all of us and it's my fault.'

I want to kick myself for responding but the rawness of it bursts out of me. My hands shake and it's out there now, in the room with us.

'Our perception of things can be wrong, you know,' he says, leaning back on his chair. 'We don't know if that boy was drunk and out of control. We don't know his intention – if there was any.'

I was there, Malcolm, you absolute gowl. 'How do you mean?' I say.

He steeples his long thin fingers. 'Catastrophic thinking.' He says this like it's the answer to a really hard question on *University Challenge*. Phrase of the day. He's delighted with himself.

'You're traumatised. You haven't dealt with the grief from your mother's death. Then the suicide on top of that – you expect the worst, Saoirse. It's a symptom of your PTSD.'

'But the worst has happened. Mam is dead. Finn is dead. Cian could have died.'

My voice is small. I'm almost afraid to challenge his phrase of the day.

'Perception, Saoirse. You see yourself as a catalyst – as an instigator. You're a great girl, you've just had a bad couple of years. It's not your fault.'

I stretch my face to stop myself bawling. Crying makes it worse. Letting it out makes it real and then it hurts. My breathing is ragged.

'From the diaphragm, Saoirse. Like this.'

He holds his stomach and takes these exaggerated breaths. I copy him. We stay like this for a while, the room filled with our synchronised rhythmic breathing.

'That's it. See? It works. You need to practise this. Every time you feel ... overcome ... you need to do this exercise. I promise it will help.'

I keep up the breathing, just to show him what a good patient I am. It's easier than talking.

'Things will get better with time. Your grief has doubled but it will ease. That's it, Saoirse. You have a lovely rhythm going.'

At least I'm good at breathing. Shit at everything else but good at the old inhalation and exhalation.

'I'd like to see you on a weekly basis for the next while. I think you need it. Are you happy with that?'

I nod. Inhale. Exhale. He checks his watch. Smiles. Session over. Thank fuck for that. I think I passed the normal-reaction test.

'I will see you next Friday. What time suits?'

'Is five o'clock available? I've work.'

'Yes. That's no problem. You're doing well, Saoirse.'

I smile as I leave. The room feels cold.

Outside, the sun whitens and bleaches the street, making it look exotic and not the shithole that it really is. A dog sits in the doorway of the hairdresser's, tongue hanging out, panting. He knows how to do the breathing thing. I feel drunk. It's hard work pretending to be normal. My stomach hurts. I walk up the street, feeling dizzy and sick. Traffic snails past, car after car heading home from the beach.

I'm at the top of Main Street when I spot her. Megan.

She's crossing over to my side of the road, in cut-off shorts and a tiny pink T-shirt. She weaves between the cars and somebody blows a horn at her. She looks straight at me but her eyes are glassy, like Timber's after a long session. She's drunk or high or both. She wanders down an alleyway and I follow. She leans against a boarded-up house, misses the wall and stumbles to the ground. She's splayed there, knee bleeding, head back against the graffiti-covered wall. She leans forward and pukes, missing the ground, and it runs down her tee shirt in yellow ribbons.

'Are ... are you OK?' I say, kneeling next to her.

She looks at me but there's no recognition there. Her face is wet and mascara stripes her cheeks.

'No.' Her voice is whispery, like she doesn't trust it.

'Did you take something? Drink something?'

She nods.

'Which?'

She starts puking again and I hold her hair back as she empties her stomach onto the tarmac. I find a bottle of water in my bag and force her to drink some. She wipes her mouth with her hand and tries to focus her eyes on me. They won't obey.

'Molly. I took my brother's molly and Mam's good vodka. I feel ...'

The water comes up this time, clear and copious.

'Hey, Megan, you need to go home. Will I call your mam?'

She shakes her head so hard I'm afraid she'll throw up again.

'No. She's sad and she'll kill me and I don't know ...'

She leans against me, crying, her bony shoulders shaking.

'He's dead. My brother. I miss him ...'

She buries her head in my chest and her plaintive sobs fill the alley, ringing off the derelict houses and finding a timbre in the narrow street. I think of Malcolm and his phrase of the day and how fucking little he knows about pain and grief and loss. You can't learn that from a book or an online course. Megan's out of it and I don't want to make things worse for her but what if she dies? What if she needs her stomach pumped? I take out my phone and ring Dylan.

'Hey, are you still at work? Look, Megan's here and she's out of it and I don't know what to do and ... great. Granary Lane. Yeah. Thanks.'

She's still crying and buried in me which is good as it means she's alive and I can hand her over to Dylan.

'I miss him,' she says again.

'I know,' I say. 'I miss him too.'

'I took the molly he took to see if ... to see what happens,' she says.

I want to ask her what she wanted to see and my brain goes into overdrive. Did Finn take molly that night? Is that what tipped him over the edge?

'How many were there?' I say, trying to keep my voice level. 'How many?'

She shrugs and dry retches.

'How many? It's important. How many?'

'Four. In his room. I only took one,' she says, like she's been good or something.

I knew it. Jade and Nicky that night. It had to be that. It's still my fault. Dominoes. I brought Jade here.

'Hey.' Dylan's still in his lifeguard shorts and hoodie, hair damp. I can smell the sea off him. He hunkers down and shakes Megan's shoulder.

'Meg? Come on.' He's checking her eyes. 'She's drunk,' he says. 'Langers.'

'She drank vodka,' I say. 'And molly. She took molly.'

'Fucking hell. She puked it all up, though,' he says, eyeing the river of vomit across the ground. 'That's good.'

'I didn't want to ring her mother ... you know ... sorry to be landing this on you.'

'You're grand, Saoirse. She's in bits lately. Gets absolutely wasted when she goes out. Every single time. I'll bring her home.'

'Thanks,' I say.

He lifts her up and she seems a bit steadier on her feet. I take her other side and we get her to Dylan's car, double-parked on Main Street. He puts her into the back seat and she lies down, eyes closing straight away.

'How are you?' says Dylan.

I shrug. 'OK.'

'I'm away tomorrow with Mam – last thing I want to do. Meet up when I get back?'

'Sure,' I say. I'm not sure. I'm not sure of anything.

I watch as Dylan pulls away. Heat rises from the street and beats off the snail-trail of cars coming from the beach. The town feels tight and wound-up. *Things I know. My head is messed up and Malcolm doesn't help. I miss Finn. I miss his kindness, his positive outlook, his hope – ironic now – his neat-freak ways, his bad jokes. I have to get away from this weird, toxic place.*

14

The sun comes out as soon as I step off the bus, making Limerick look exotic and European and cosmopolitan. I'm at Arthur's Quay and I stroll over to the river as I know Jade'll be late. It's high tide and kayakers battle the Curragower Falls while the castle keeps guard. I inhale the river, deep Malcolm-breaths, and it's like it kickstarts my home city DNA. No tightness here. No watching eyes and interconnecting people whose family trees are a psychologist's dream. The sun's dipping over the Shannon, ready to drop, and spreads liquid gold across the water. I can feel my chest loosen and my lungs expand for the first time in months.

'Bitch! Told ya I'd be on time.'

Jade's walking across the park, a black mirage in the sunshine. Her hair is pink today and she's wearing a tight black jumpsuit with a maroon leather jacket. She must be melting.

'You're half an hour late.'

She crosses her eyes. 'So, Mam's party is at eight – your nana's there now, decorating the place and swamping gins – fuck. I told you to bring your guitar. Mam wants you to play Johnny Cash. So Nicky's coming later. Wait until you see the brothers, Saoirse – fucking giants – like four Paul O'Connells. I swear, you'd need a trough to feed them. Anyway – I have a plan.'

I'm caught up already in Jade's mad energy. 'I dread your plans.'

She grins. 'I found a fella for you.'

'Oh fuck.'

'Yep. Luke. A genius – guess what his pet subject is? Guess ... guess ...'

'I don't want a fella, Jade, seriously.'

'The brain. He's as obsessed as you. He's a first year in UL – studying ... am ... something I can't remember, something complicated. Which reminds me: I was drunk filling out my CAO form – I haven't a clue what I applied for. So yeah. Come on.'

'Are we not going to Nana's first? I want to drop off my backpack.'

She doesn't even hear me. She's marching down the path towards the castle. I have to run to catch up with her. She's talking away, not realising I'm behind. This is exactly what I needed. Distraction, familiarity, belonging. Minus the fella. She can keep him. I want to get wasted. We've reached the castle, and Jade sits down on the sloping grass verge and pats the space next to her. I sit down beside her and she pulls off her backpack.

'Bag of cans – literally,' she says, handing me one. 'It's shite but they were on offer,' she says, popping the can and slugging it back. 'Thought we'd need a drink before we face a fiftieth party, and anyway – this is my new favourite spot. Do you like it?'

She talks about it like it's a new outfit. I pop a can and take a warm sip of beer. 'It's perfect, Jade, just perfect. I needed a dose of home.'

She takes out a vape and puffs on it. 'How are things back there? Sorry I didn't get down.'

'I know. You told me every time you rang.'

'Please get rid of your brick phone. I can't send you messages or, more importantly, memes or gifs.'

I watch a swan family gliding on the river. 'I don't know. I prefer life without the constant social media shit, you know? Especially with ... all that happened.'

'Yeah. Cian. Fucking gowl. If he hadn't jumped, I'd have pushed him in,' she says.

I punch her arm. 'Lousy!' I don't mention the Megan incident. It's too private or something.

'So stoked you're here. It must be a year?'

'About that,' I say, playing with the can. The beer is vile. Undrinkable.

She leans into me and catches my hand. 'I missed you, Saoirse, and your bonkers head.'

'Same.'

She leans forward and roots in the bag again. 'Ta-da!'

She holds up two old Coke bottles filled with a peachy liquid. 'MiWadi?'

'Vodka – only mixer I could find was a drop of mango juice. It's mostly vodka and you have to drink it. All of it. We can't be going into all those auld wans stone cold sober, like. We'll do it like shots – ready?'

She hands me a bottle and we both drink together. She's right, it's mostly vodka and it catches my throat and makes me shudder. I like it.

'Next one,' she says.

We have it downed in three attempts.

'Here he is,' says Jade, jumping to her feet and running towards a tall black lad in a salmon-coloured hoodie. Even from here he is gorgeous – or else I have vodka eyes. I stand up too and watch while they hug. 'Aboy the kid! This is Saoirse, I told you about her.'

He smiles at me. 'I'm Luke. And ignore Jade – I know she's trying to set us up, like – she thinks we're thirteen.'

I laugh and he grins at me.

'Let's go – we're, like, late already,' says Jade and she's off running her marathon up Nicholas Street and across Thomond Bridge.

❊   ❊   ❊

'Play us Johnny Cash,' says Nana from across the room. 'Saoirse, come on. I told them all how good you are – don't make a show of me.'

I pretend I don't hear her. Jade's over talking to Nicky. I think they're fighting. And Jade's mam, Annie, is up jiving with her four giant sons. I'm busy listening to Luke.

'Ignore her. Keep going,' I say to Luke. He's telling me about mind cloning.

'Jaysus. I can't. It'll fry your brain.'

'Try me,' I say.

'OK. OK. Here's the challenge. How do we go from a physical substrate of cells, which are connected inside our heads, to our mental world – like our thoughts, our feelings, our memories?'

I take a sip of beer. 'Haven't a clue.'

'I'll try to tell you in simple language. Let's pretend the brain is a computer. It turns inputs, sensory data, into outputs – like our behaviour. Computation.'

'I'm with you.'

'If the brain could be mapped – all the complex connections of all the neurons – they are what encodes information – make us who we are – and we could copy this, code it, then ...'

'Geek Silicon Valley stuff,' I say.

'Not really. You see, the computer is not important: the *data* is. My data. Your data. That's what makes us who we are. Most computers will be able to run an accurate simulation of the human mind within the next few years.'

'Yeah. Moore's Law and all that,' I say. 'I don't believe it.'

'In order to upload, though, you need to download first, to decipher the data. Mind uploading.'

I laugh. 'Fantasy.'

'It's happening already. All the big tech companies, all over the world. They're all investing in this. In mind cloning, mind uploading.'

I watch his face, intense and confident. He reminds me of Sheila, my brilliant English teacher, talking about William Blake. She thought Blake was a visionary. I thought he had too many bad trips.

'Forget AI, mind cloning will be the next big thing – digital versions of humans that can live for ever with mind files – a place to store all aspects of our personality – run on a software for consciousness. We have the potential to have radically extended life spans. Radically extended cognitive abilities. Think of it like a disembodied mind, Saoirse.' He laughs, slugs back his pint. 'Another?'

'Yep. I need it after that. Why, though? Why would you, like, want to live for ever? Wouldn't you be bored out of your tree?'

He laughs again. 'Money and power.'

I'm admiring him at the bar when Nana presents herself, complete with a guitar.

'Yer man said he needs a break and I told him you'd play and it's Annie's birthday so get up there – you're hanging out of that fella all night.'

She pulls me up and I make my way to the tiny stage. I'm mortified. Nana isn't.

'That's my granddaughter, Saoirse, wait till ye hear her, lads, better than ... than ... Lizzo.'

She shouts this to the whole party and I can feel blood rising up my face. I climb onto the stool and tune the guitar while wondering how Nana knows Lizzo. I feel woozy but in a good way and I launch into 'Ring of Fire' and give it wellie. I'm watching Luke out of the corner of my eye and

I can see the shock on his face. Good shock, I think. I follow straight away with 'Walk the Line' and they're all up on the floor dancing, even Jade. Nicky's in the corner talking to two young women. Gowl.

I finish my set and ignore Nana's screams for more. I sit back down with Luke and take a gulp of Guinness.

'Thirsty work,' I say.

'You were amazing, Saoirse.'

'Brain fried?'

He leans into me and kisses me on the mouth. Fuck. That was fast. It's the female guitarist effect. Works both ways.

'Fuck – I'm sorry – I ... I should have asked if it was OK, like,' he says.

I want to kiss him back for saying that. 'You're grand. I'm just not ... in that place right now.'

'Break-up?'

'Something like that.'

I'm watching Nicky flirting and I'm not the only one. One of Jade's brothers is staring over at him. Nicky's oblivious. Jade sees too and her brother is talking to her.

'You used to live in Limerick, right? Jade was telling me, you know, about your mam and that.'

'Yep.' Jade has gone over to Nicky and she's agitated, shouting. People are turning to look. One of her brothers is cracking his knuckles. Nicky grabs Jade by the arm and pulls her out to the patio area, fronting the river. My stomach's erupting and I'm glad of the bad music. I have that feeling again, that curve balls are flying and looking to land.

'Excuse me,' I say, as the voices rise on the patio. I go out and stand in the doorway. The brother's there already.

'I'll bate the head off that Nicky yoke in a minute,' he says. 'What a gowl of a fella – watch him – with his smooth talk and his baldy head. I'll be dug out of him, like.'

'John ...'

'James.'

'James, she can handle herself.'

'Why are you talking to them, like, for the whole night?' Jade shouts at Nicky.

Nicky's voice is calm. 'Jade, you're irrational, calm yourself down – this is so childish. I'm just being sociable, that's all.'

'You're the child – trying to make me jealous, fucking gowl,' she says.

'Jade. Calm down. Be reasonable – my job involves talking to people ...'

'Sure – talking to two young wans ...'

'There's irony there in that, Jade. Come on, babe, you're better than this.'

'Shut up,' says Jade. 'I know what I saw.'

There's a full audience now. Nana's brought her gin and all and grabbed the best view.

'Jade. We talked about this. About your ... your imagination getting the better of you. It's in your head, babe.'

Jade's mother, Annie, is trying to hold James back. But it's Jade who strikes: raising her fist, she punches Nicky on the shoulder, not even hard, and he hits the floor like he's feigning for a penalty. James pulls Nicky up and they're in a whisper conversation in the corner. It's all over in sixty seconds but I feel I've been watching it in slo-mo. People have their phones out, videoing it.

'Put your fucking phones away,' I shout. They train their phones on me, waiting for another episode.

James and Nicky are best buds now, deep in conversation, James lapping up Nicky's bullshit. Jade's just standing there, head down. I make my way towards her and put my arm around her shoulder. She's shaking. James comes over, all smiles.

'He's pure sound, like – Jaysus, Jade, you're some woman for the drama,' he says.

I look over at Nicky, leaning against the wall, pint in hand. Our eyes lock. He knows I know what he is.

'Want a drink? I'm going to the bar,' says Nicky.

Jade takes off, flying down the road, and I follow. I run parallel to the river but I can't see her. I reach Sarsfield Bridge and think that she must have gone in the other direction. My face is slick with sweat and my stomach's a bubble of anxiety, mixed with vodka and Guinness. I lean on the bridge wall to force air into my lungs. I take out my phone and ring her. No answer. I'm watching the river like it knows something I don't, watching the black current being sucked under the bridge and out to the estuary. I think of Mam for the first time today. I think of her Three Bridges walk that she used to drag us on, her obsession with the river, the black powerful artery that cuts right through the city, taking things with it. Rubbish, old bikes, tyres, lives.

I jog back to the pub, phone glued to my ear as I redial. She's sitting on the wall, facing the Treaty Stone, crying.

I can hear her sobs from way back. Three people in high-vis gear surround her. I break into a run. They're the Suicide Watch team, who patrol the river on a voluntary basis.

'Saoirse, will you tell these gowls I'm just upset, I'm not going to throw myself into the Shannon over a fella – are ye joking, like?'

'She's with me,' I tell them. 'She's fine. She just had a fight with her boyfriend,' I say, and they move off, walkie-talkies crackling.

I sit down beside her, linking her arm with mine.

'I'm not going to top myself,' she says, wiping her eyes with her sleeve.

'I know.'

'I saw him talking all night to those two and I lost it – that's all. He's right. I'm kind of crazy – all over the place and he's so mature and –'

'Hey. That's not true.'

'It is. I can't ... I can't manage being with someone – they always end up dumping me.'

'Jade, stop being so hard on yourself. You're the funniest, most out-there person I know.'

'Yeah, but that's part of it, you see. Out there. Rainbow hair, tattoos, piercings, I've got nothing without them. Like you're really smart, interesting, you sing. Fellas like that. The other choice is to be an airhead and I'm way too mouthy for that and ... it's just fucking hard, isn't it?'

'I'm a mess too, Jade. It's like ... it's like we're all having tiny breakdowns all the time.'

I can't believe that I'm quoting Dylan to her. I wish he was here.

'I'll be fine. It was my fault.' She takes out her vape and puffs. The air is pungent with chemical sweetness.

'And fuck my brother – hanging on Nicky's every word – and anyway I can protect myself. I don't need the four of them watching me – it's like being out on remand. Fuckers.'

'It wasn't your fault. It was his.'

She looks at me, eyes still wet, pink fringe pushed to one side. She doesn't know how beautiful she is. She really doesn't. She shakes her head. 'My fault. I'm always annoying him, getting on his nerves and he's ...' She examines my face. 'Say it – say what you're thinking, Saoirse.'

'I ... I'm not thinking anything.'

'You don't know him like I do,' she says.

She leans against me, arm around my shoulder, in the shadow of the Treaty Stone, river roaring behind us. I can hear somebody in the pub singing a painful medley of Springsteen songs.

'Stay in mine tonight? Be like old times – we can watch movies and bitch about everyone.'

'Yep. Nana's pissed – she won't miss me at all.'

'Right. I've a plan,' says Jade.

'Oh fuck, another one?'

She's up and crossing the road to the pub and shouting and waving to Suicide Watch across the riverfront.

15

I have to rescue Luke from Nana's clutches. She has him up waltzing and is killing him for not knowing how. He's a very handsome lad but he'll never be a dancer. He's all angles and edges. We have to wait for the cake-cutting before we can leave and they really should have planned that part better. The cake – in the shape of a dodgy look-ing Thomond Park – does not survive a drunken fall by Jade's youngest brother and loses the east stand before it reaches the table. Jade drags us away as soon as the candles are blown out.

'They're all wrecked,' she says as the three of us spill onto the pavement outside. 'Your nana's a howl, Saoirse, I was going to bring her with us. She said she'll see us in the morning for a fry-up. Actually, do you know what? I'm starving – pit-stop in Chicken Hut?'

'What about Nicky?' I say.

'He told his new pal James that he had to leave – that he'd sort me out later.'

'What does that even mean?'

Jade laughs. 'You're more paranoid than me – it means we'll sort out the fight, that's all.'

She's tearing down the road and across the bridge, forcing myself and Luke to run after her. The city's Friday-night busy, gaggles of young people going to bars and clubs and I'm comparing it in my head to Cloughmore and the dozy street and the sound of a squeeze box and the rise and dip of pub conversations.

'Do you want food?' says Luke as we reach the chipper.

'No – I ate at the party,' I say. 'Jesus, watch her – she's ordering the whole menu, including the server.'

'That's Jade,' says Luke. 'I wish I was more like her. You know – she doesn't care what anyone thinks – she ... owns herself, like.'

'So, what are you like?'

He laughs. 'A nerd, but I pretend I'm not. I can't even own that.'

'How do you know Jade?'

'I play rugby with her brother – John, the big guy.'

'They're all big.'

'True.'

'Do you like it? Rugby?'

He smiles. 'I like watching it. Playing it is terrifying. I love Gaelic football, but you know what it's like around here – it's rugby or hurling or nothing.'

'You'd do well in Cloughmore – they're mad for Gaelic football there. My dad calls it Gaelic volleyball. Hates the game – pure Limerick man.'

'I know Cloughmore – you pass it going to the beach near the cliffs.'

'Yeah, it's a passing-through kind of town. Will you look at Jade and the huge bag of food – what is she up to at all?'

Jade arrives out, still talking over her shoulder to the server.

'Come on, let's go,' she says, and we're back to running down O'Connell Street, chasing Jade with her giant bag of food. She stops at Sarsfield Bridge and scans the river.

'Is this what we're doing for the night?' I say. 'Running around Limerick?'

'They're they are,' she says and runs down the steps towards the quay. She's found the Suicide Watch lads and she's handing out bags of chips to them. We watch from the bridge and I'm thinking of Finn and how he'd do the exact same thing and I feel a gnawing belt of something in my chest that makes my eyes water. She turns to wave at me and grins, and the pain hurts even more. My face is wet and I'm standing there on the bridge like an eejit next to a lad with a god's body and a nerd's brain and she's hurtling up the steps and I hug her so tight she squeals.

'Mind my gravy chip, gowl,' she says but stays in the hug.

She pulls away. 'Right. Party in Riverpoint. Wait till ye see this apartment – penthouse, like, and all glass. Come on.'

Another race down the quays and we're going up the lift in a swanky tower block overlooking the river. Jade's shoving chips into her mouth like somebody's going to steal them from her, and Luke's laughing, and everything feels right.

*　　*　　*

The apartment's stunning – glass and reflections and smoke and mirrors and you don't know where the glass ends and the water begins. The crowd are older than us and I don't see Nicky first in the cluster of new faces. Somebody hands me a drink and I edge towards the balcony, Luke following. Nicky's holding court in the centre of the room. There are lines of coke lined up on the table and Jade goes for it, balling her chip bag on the way and depositing it in a plant pot. Luke's met somebody he knows and is chatting away. Jade's now sitting on Nicky's knee, kissing his bald head and calling him love names, and the sleeping black fist in my stomach rises up my throat, bursting to get out. I swallow it back down and sip my drink – some sugary concoction that's sickening and delicious at the same time.

'Sit down, Saoirse,' says Nicky, patting the free seat beside him on the long leather couch. 'Welcome to my pad.'

His fucking apartment. I sit and fiddle with my drink.

'Good party, yeah?' he says.

'Just got here,' I say.

Jade's still kissing him and he looks like a mafia boss with a moll hanging out of him. I hate this guy. Soft music plays from surround-sound speakers. I can feel Nicky's eyes on me and I'm willing Luke to come over, but no chance – he's deep into the chat. I look everywhere but at Nicky because I can feel that electric curve ball in the air, waiting to land somewhere. And I don't trust the fist of anger in my belly.

'Want a line?' he says, forcing me to look at him. He's stroking Jade's back and her butt and I want to punch him

154

so hard it hurts. He's doing it on purpose, annoying me. Teasing me.

I shake my head. 'No. I'm grand with the drink,' I say. My voice is shaky and he thinks it's nerves, but it's cold, black hate. Jade gets up and walks away, abandoning me to this gowl. He inches closer to me. I want to puke on him. Denise Chaila starts to play, and Jade's dancing in the middle of the floor. Nicky's winking at me and laughing – like we are in cahoots together.

'How are all your bogger friends?' He's rolling a spliff as he talks.

'Fine.'

'You're very uptight. Do you ever smile?'

'Only when I'm happy,' I say. I slug back my drink in one go and reach for another on the side table. I don't know who owns it but I need it more than them.

Jade stumbles and sprawls on the floor, laughing. A tall blond man helps her up and she staggers and knocks a beer bottle. The liquid fizzes on the cream carpet.

'You're wasted, Jade, sit down – I'll clean this mess up,' Nicky says.

Jade sinks into a leather recliner, watching the beer stain grow. Nicky's back with sponge and spray and makes a big show of cleaning the stain, smiling at Jade and then laughing and shaking his head. Bastard.

'Take it easy there, Jade,' he says. 'You've had a ... what's the word? Dramatic – yep – dramatic night,' he says.

A couple of his college pals, hairy unshaven PhD types, laugh.

My black fist is up and out before I know what's happening.

'Shut the fuck up,' I say, but it's a shout and everybody turns towards us. Nicky's grinning, big dopey head on him. I'm clenching my fists and trying to sit on them.

'OK. Can we just chill, Saoirse? Can we just calm down? No need to bite my ear off,' he says, and his friends laugh.

I look around for Luke and can see him out on the balcony, still talking to the same lad. I catch his attention and wave, thinking it might bring him in. He just waves back and returns to his conversation. Jade's talking to a young lad with rust-coloured hair in a Radiohead T-shirt. He's laughing and kneels beside her chair. Their heads are bent together, a rust and pink mesh as they whisper and laugh. I nearly want to cheer her on. I sneak a look at Nicky and there it is. Rage. Jealousy. Fury. I sink back into the couch, enjoying this turn of events. Jade's animated, her hands flying, and Rust Head's cracking up. Perfect.

'Jade?' says Nicky, voice soft and coaxing.

She doesn't hear him. Good woman, Jade.

'Jade.'

He's more urgent now. She looks over at him but continues her chat.

'Can you come here, please?' says Nicky.

Jade's too engrossed in her storytelling to hear him.

'Jade. I want to talk to you,' Nicky says.

I can hear the edge in his voice, feel it in the air.

'Calm down, Nicky. She's ... you know ... just socialising ... being friendly,' I say, smiling at him.

He's about to reply but Luke comes in and sits beside me. Nicky takes out his phone and Jade's phone pings. She ignores it.

'She doesn't even like you,' Nicky says, looking at me.

I shrug. 'Seems she doesn't like you either.'

'I love this song,' says Jade, pulling Rust Hair up for a dance.

Nicky kills the music with a remote. There's an awkward moment, Jade and Rust Hair frozen in dance poses and conversations hanging mid-air.

'This is weird,' whispers Luke.

'Put on the music – I love that track,' says Jade, trying to wrestle the remote from Nicky's hand.

He's pretending it's a joke, the sneaky fucker.

'Give it to me,' says Jade. 'I was dancing to that.'

Nicky holds the remote above his head. She tries to grab it, and he play fights with her, teasing her with the stupid remote. We're all there watching and I'm swallowing bile and trying to compose myself. It doesn't work.

I stand up, straighten my dress and pour the blue cocktail over Nicky's baldy head, his snow-white T-shirt, his deep-pile cream carpet. The blue liquid makes a much better shape on the floor than the beer. Lovely contrast. He stands up, dripping more of the cocktail onto the carpet. I grab the remote and Denise Chaila's singing in the background and I'm enjoying his face, his drippy blue face and tiny, mean eyes.

'You should clean that up or it'll leave an awful stain,' I say and drop the glass on the floor.

'You need help,' he says. 'You're bonkers. Crazy. You bit a guy's ear off, for fuck sake.'

I walk right up to him and twang his ear. 'Yep. That's me.'

He pushes my hand away and I lose my balance and fall, hitting my hip on the edge of the coffee table.

'Get out,' he says. 'You're mad. No wonder ye lot are topping yourselves in that shithole you're from. Fucking crazy.'

'Pleasure,' I say. I walk out, and Jade follows me into the hallway.

'What was that about, Saoirse?'

'It was about him being an absolute dick. What are you doing with a creep like that?'

She leans against the wall, twiddling her nose ring. 'It was just a bit of fun, and you went mad.'

'You can't see it, can you?'

'See what?'

'Oh, please. You're better than this Jade, than him.'

'Stop it. Stop being all judgey. Fuck sake – why are you so serious? Can't you ever just have a laugh?'

Nicky's in the doorway, smiling.

'You OK, babe?' he says, reaching for Jade. She curls into him.

'Are you coming, Jade? I'm staying at yours,' I say, turning for the door.

'She's staying with me,' Nicky says, slapping her on the arse and whistling as he walks away.

'Gowl,' I say to his back. He throws me the finger.

'Loony,' he says and disappears through the door.

'Nice lad there, Jade. Hang on to him.'

'Oh fuck off and lighten up, Saoirse.'

'Grand. Good luck,' I say, opening the door. 'There's just one thing. One question.' I turn and look at her and I see tiny Jade, six-year-old Jade, arguing with teachers because she can't wear trousers like the boys, jaw stuck out, eyes defiant. 'How many molly did you give Finn that night? I need to know.'

She laughs. A mean, dirty laugh. 'Oh, here we go – let's blame somebody, anybody, for Finn. Anybody but you.'

'What's that supposed to mean?'

'You're miserable. Nicky says you'd make anyone depressed. There's a misery vibe off you, like, all the time.'

'Fuck you,' I say and open the door for the second time. I walk towards the lift and she's behind me.

'Five. Ten. Fifteen. What number would you like? What number fixes it for you? Happy now? Does that bring him back?'

I watch her face disappear as the lift doors close. My body has the shakes, like it was waiting for refuge before giving up. *Things I know. If I'd had a knife in my hand I would have gone for Nicky. I could easily be a murderer. I've lost Jade too.*

16

'Hey. Wait up.'

I turn around and there's Luke pounding across the road, my backpack in his hand.

He gulps air and hands it to me.

'I heard the ... the fight in the hallway and I didn't want to butt in and then you were gone ... so ...'

Thanks,' I say, taking the bag. 'That's nice of you.' I slip the bag on my back and march down the street, scrunching my eyes so I don't cry. The night sky is spitting rain, like a trailer for the real thing, and there's a word for the smell when rain falls after a dry spell and I can't think of it and that small thing makes me hate myself.

'Hey – where are you staying?' he says. 'I'll walk you home.'

'I'm fine.'

'It's late and ... it's not a problem.'

'I was supposed to stay in Jade's.'

'I know. You can stay in mine. My parents are gone to Kilkee – to the mobile.'

I don't have a key to Nana's, and even if I had, I don't want to face her questions. She likes her gin but she still doesn't miss a trick.

'What if you're a serial killer?'

'I'll make it quick – I promise.'

I smile and I don't want to be alone tonight – even hanging out with a serial killer is better than that.

'He's a dick – I hate him.' We're at the top of Mulgrave Street and I know there's a mural here that I want to see and I still can't think of that word and instead collective nouns jump around in my head. *A sloth of bears. A brood of hens. A colony of gulls. A stud of horses.*

'He's a gowl. I've told Jade that over and over but there's no talking to her,' he says. 'The more you tell Jade she shouldn't do something, the more she'll want to.'

'Look,' I say, standing in front of the mural.

'A woman with a pram full of dogs,' he says, stepping on to the road to get a better view. 'I've seen it already but haven't a clue who she is ... or the dogs for that matter.'

'Dodo Reddan. A Limerick legend. My nana knew her. She took in stray dogs and pushed them around town in the pram ... and she took them to rugby matches. She was mad into the rugby. I never met her but I love her.'

My eyes are wet and I'm crying in front of a lad I barely know about Dodo Reddan – a woman I never met – and I know that if I can think of that one word that my brain will settle. I walk towards the mural and press my face against it. I imagine I can still smell the paint, feel the brush strokes on my skin. For no reason at all, Mam pops into my head – she's on a red bike with a basket and wearing shorts and a blue spotted top. She's young, maybe even my age, and she's smiling and I don't know if this is a photo I saw of her or my imagination.

'How does memory work?' I say to the mural.

'Jaysus, that's random,' Luke says.

'Do you know?'

'I fucking love memory – incredible feat of engineering. Like it sits inside the medial temporal lobe and its most impressive function is its filing system. Better than anything a supercomputer could do,' says Luke.

Dodo Reddan's looking down on the two of us looking up at her.

'Yeah, Luke, but when we remember something, we're not actually recalling the original event. We're remembering the last time we remembered it ...' I wipe my face and snotty nose with my sleeve and the words keep spilling out of me. 'So we're constantly wiping our pasts and editing a new one that makes sense to us now – do you get me, Luke? We're creating one that makes sense to us now, in the present.'

'It's going to flog – let's go,' he says.

'Which means all memories are, by definition, alive. Do you follow me? They change and we change them – it's human nature.'

'Saoirse ...'

'I've been thinking about this – a kind of subconscious thinking, you know, like it's bubbling there underneath the surface and ...'

I lose my train of thought and struggle to clear my head. I feel funny and am wondering if there was an extra something in that blue cocktail. 'We can project guilt back onto an event that was in fact perfectly innocent – a kind of less extraordinary truth ...'

'You're shivering, Saoirse.'

'Yeah, but I'm kind of happy. I'd forgotten all that memory stuff and when you know the logistics of something – how stuff works – then it's easier to ...'

I want to say, *Not remember. Dismiss a memory. Forget. Disown.* Instead I shrug.

'Come on,' says Luke. 'The heavens are about to open.'

And they do, in *Angela's Ashes* fashion, as Nana would say. We run down the street holding hands as the rain lashes us and there's a freedom and madness in it and I don't realise I'm screaming until I see the look on Luke's face. I smile at him to reassure him that I'm not bonkers or crazy or a vampire.

His house is a red-brick terrace in the shadow of St Mary's Cathedral. It's chocolate-box pretty, rose arch over the door, old-fashioned windows, flower boxes. He goes in but I stand outside, awkward and shy. Maybe I should go home and try to wake up Nana.

'Come in,' he calls.

I follow him through the hallway and into the living room. Family portraits stare at me from the walls: mother, father, two children, all staring. I back out of the room.

'I've to go,' I say and run but I can't get the front door open and he's behind me.

'I'll open it for you, Saoirse. I'm not going to hurt you.'

'I know. It's just ... just everything and I want my nana and ...' I lean against him and he puts his long arms around me, weighting me down, anchoring me, and then I let go and cry and I can't stop and if I think of that one word it'll help me, I know it will, and my stomach's gurgling and I want to sleep and never wake up ... that's not true. It isn't true and I want Dylan and his familiarity and his golden light everywhere or is that just an edited memory of how Dylan is and ... we're walking upstairs. More family portraits, more stares from the walls. He opens a door and pulls me onto a bed. It has an astronomy quilt cover – Pluto and Venus and Saturn floating across the bed – and I don't want this at all, but I want the weight of him to pull me down. To anchor me. He strips off my clothes, everything except my knickers and bra. He walks over to the wardrobe, and I can hear the dawn chorus, and if I close my eyes I could be in Cloughmore with Eva snoring across from me and ...

'Here,' he says, handing me a white T-shirt. It smells of lemon. 'Put that on.'

I sit up, confused, and pull the T-shirt on over my head. He has a towel and he's rubbing my hair with it and patting my face. I lie back against the pillow and watch as he strips down to his boxers and collects the wet clothes. He sits on the bed, and I reach out for him, pulling his face towards mine because I need the weight of him and still the word won't come. He pulls the duvet up to my chin.

'See you in the morning,' he says.

'Stay with me.'

He looks at me. 'Not a good idea.'

'Why? Because I'm bonkers? Crazy? Afraid I'll bite your ear off? I get it, Luke. Off you go. Fuck off.'

He pulls me into him and the tears come again and I want to have my tear ducts removed or whatever it is in the brain that makes me cry and I stroke his head, or else it's the pillow, and sink back into it or him, I don't know if I'm awake or dreaming, and there it is in my head and it's beautiful. The word. *Petrichor*. The unique earthy smell associated with rain. That's in my dream. Not Mam. Not Finn. Just that beautiful word.

* * *

I open my eyes. A thin crack of light inches through the curtains and lasers me as I sit up. Last night is a jumble of images in my head, little mad pop-ups of blue drinks and a mural and Luke and ... and Jade. I creep out of bed and see my clothes from last night folded neatly on a chair. I can smell the Lenor as I dress myself. Soft cotton. Mam's brand. Dad is more of an Aldi man. I grab my backpack and open the door. All clear. I tiptoe down the stairs and tackle the front door. It glides open and I close it softly behind me. Outside I take in lungfuls of morning air, heavy with the smell of the river and roses from the garden. I dry-heave into a flowerpot by the gate and walk the opposite way to Nana's house. It's like my legs have their own satnav. The river is alive and heaving its way through the city, forcing itself under bridges and locks and out into the estuary and freedom.

It's spitting rain by the time I get there and nothing has changed and everything has. There's the tree outside my window that scrapes the glass on stormy nights. There're my initials on the footpath, carved when workers came and dug up the roads. There's a trail of paw prints too and this makes me cry out. I'd forgotten about Stormy, my old dog and the best boy that ever lived. The memories come now, his big golden head, the earthy smell of him, the sight of him on the road after our stupid neighbour hit him with her brand-new fancy car. I should have brought his bones down to Cloughmore when we moved, I should have dug him up and taken him with me and ... and Mam too. We left Mam behind in some ugly vast graveyard with no trees on the edge of the city. I lean against the tree, watching the house. They've concreted over the whole front garden with that pretend paving and Dad's wildflower garden is gone. He loved that piece of wilderness and the neighbours hated it. There's no car in the driveway and the house seems silent. I sneak into the drive and open the side gate. I want to see our back garden, all Dad's wonderful plants, his raised beds of vegetables and flowers, our small city orchard, the slope from the back door that we rolled down when we were small. It's like I woke up, craving memories.

The garden is gone, replaced by an ugly, oversized glass-box extension and more paving. Stormy's bones are now encased in concrete. Fuck sake. Mam's magnolia tree is still there and I bury my head in its foliage, willing the memories to rise. They don't. They're all erased. Rewritten. I walk over to the extension and peer in. Everything of ours has been obliterated. Doors. Floors. Even walls. The vast room is white, sleek and soulless. I press my face against the glass, desperately looking for something that's familiar. That's ours. A blaring noise erupts throughout the house, pinging my ears. I can feel the glass tremor through my face, but I'm glued there, cocooned by the blaring alarm.

'Excuse me?' a voice says from over the wall next door. 'What are you doing?'

'I ... I don't know,' I say. 'I don't know.'

'Saoirse? Saoirse Considine?'

I nod. It's Mr Griffin, our elderly neighbour, lover of Stormy the dog and collector of exotic plants, and he holds all the memories and they come too fast for me to process and I think my brain is fucked up from the blue drink and Jade and Mam and most of all Finn, and I run. I run so hard my legs ache and my breaths are gulps of jagged air and I never want to stop running.

17

I love Nana's house. It's terraced and stands guard over the river, windows like eyes, watching everything. Archie Cat's glaring at me from the front step and I notice that he's gained a few extra pounds. I tie up my sweat- drenched hair and Malcolm-breathe until my head settles. I'm half-hoping that Jade'll show up, that she'll be inside already, sitting with Nana, drinking strong tea and reading the hole off the neighbours. I ring the bell, Archie Cat refusing to move.

'There you are, love,' says Nana as she opens the door.

She's in a pink tracksuit and Nike runners and she doesn't look at all like she downed a pile of gins last night.

'Where's Jade? I've cooked a big fry-up – you're not still a vegetarian, are you? I got the good sausages and all from Tom's Butchers, all the way out in Castletroy. Come in, love, come in.'

I step over Archie Cat and go into the spotless hallway and through to the small kitchen.

'Jade had to work ... she says she's sorry,' I say and Nana narrows her eyes at me. She doesn't miss a trick.

'Sit yourself down there. I hope you're hungry – fried potatoes and all. You loved them when you were small – pure Irish kid, shovelling them into you ...'

Nana stops and pulls me in for a hug and I realise she's crying.

'Nana – are you OK? What's up?'

'Ah, look, 'tis nothing only Marie has a touch of leukaemia and she called earlier to tell me and, Jaysus, we're all dying off, but Marie's ... you know ... Marie's my buddy ... like you and Jade.'

I hug Nana tight and ease her down on a chair. I pour us two cups of strong tea and ignore the spread of rashers and sausages and pudding on the table.

'I'll be grand, Saoirse, 'tis the shock, like. Wasn't last night great? They all loved you singing. What time's Jade done work? Because I'm making a stew and she loves a bit of stew.'

'I don't know – she didn't say.'

'Eat up – here, I'll fill a plate for you.'

She piles a plate with food and my stomach reacts to the meat smell, gurgling and threatening to erupt.

'You're fierce pale, love. And very thin. Are you anorexic? That's gone very common these days – you know you can tell me – although your mother was very scrawny too so it could be in the genes. An appetite like a mouse she had and she wasn't even a vagan or whatever you call it.'

She's buttering bread and digging into the sausages. I feel exhausted and am struggling to keep my eyes open. She eyes me up and down.

'What's going on?'

I shake my head. 'Just tired. Late night and all that.'

'You can tell me, you know.'

'I know.'

'Are you gay, love? I often thought that – you know – with yourself and Jade being so tight and all and sure if you are that's grand. Marie's youngest is gay – it's all the go now.'

I almost laugh at this.

'Are you having another episode? You know – like that big one you had after your mother ...'

'No. I'm fine.'

She stirs her tea and I can see her going through her Saoirse-list in her head.

'Your father told me you're going to the debs – we'll make a big occasion out of it and that Dylan fella's a lovely boy except his mother can't cut hair – ruined mine last year – gave me an auld wan's style.'

How did Dad know about the debs? Eva? Small town news bulletin?

'I don't want to go,' I say.

'Go 'way outta that. 'Course you're going – We'll go shopping for the dress – the lot of us. Bit of normality after all the madness and your mother – she'd be so proud ...' Her eyes well up again. 'I don't know what's wrong with me at all today, love. My bladder's very near my eyes.'

She dabs her face with a tissue and horses into the fry-up. 'Aren't you going to eat anything, love?'

'I don't eat meat, Nan. You know that.'

'I've a bit of fish in the fridge – I could –'

'I don't eat fish either, Nan – nothing with a face.'

'Have a few spuds so,' she says, piling fried potato onto a side dish.

I pick at the food, pushing it around the plate.

'You need to cheer up – that's why you've no appetite,' she says.

Nana's really hitting all the targets today.

'I'm very tired. I need to lie down for a while.'

'Go on into the living room and take the couch, pet. I've my yoga anyway in the community centre except it makes me fart so much and the way they look at you – it isn't my fault, like. I wouldn't give it to say to that bitch down the road. I'll show up if it kills me. Remember her? The wan that kidnapped my Archie? I wish she'd go back into the convent for herself.'

My eyes are dropping at this stage and I let Nan bring me in to the couch. She layers me with throws and Archie Cat hops up and nestles into me, paws clawing at the cushions to make it comfortable for himself.

'Will I put on the telly for a bit of noise?'

I shake my head. 'I'm grand, Nana ...'

*　　*　　*

And you come. Mam. No Finn lurking around the edges of my dream. Just you. I can hear your voice and your laugh and I can smell you – I missed that smell – stay with me this time – you promised and I can't make sense of anything or anyone and I can't talk to Dad because ... because he's still sad too and poor Aran and it's all fucked up and it's not getting better like you said – it's getting worse, messier. I don't know where home is any more – none of us do – and sometimes I think you were home? You know – like the tag game we played when we were kids and that's it – you're home and we have to find you …

✱   ✱   ✱

I wake with Archie Cat curled into me, purring and snoring. I try to put order to the mess in my head but it's a melting pot of dreams and memories and real things. I can feel Mam, though, in the air, in the rush of the river across the road, in the pores of this house. There's a soft tap at the door.

'It's ready, love, the stew,' Nana says and Archie Cat stretches like a yogi – he thinks he's being called for his dinner.

'Coming.' I wander out to the kitchen, Archie trailing me. I love Nana's kitchen, the familiar table with the stripy cloth, Nana with her apron on, stirring her pots. The air is heavy with the cloying smell of meat. Nana places a bowl of stew in front of me. She has lifted the meat out and thinks I won't notice. She sits down opposite me and begins to eat. Archie Cat's watching every spoonful, head askew, eyes locked to the bowl.

'Eat up. It's all vegetinarian,' Nana says.

I stir the stew with my fork. I can see meat sinews in it.

'What's up, Saoirse?'

'The meat. I'm sorry, Nan, I can't eat the meat.'

'There's no meat in it – I took it all out,' she says. 'You'd want to be copping on – you're gone fierce skinny since you started that lark. I'd swear you're anaemic too. Look at the colour of you. You're like shit on a slate.'

I bow my head and whimper. Dry-cry into my stew. No tears. I wanted this to be great. I wanted to touch the world of my childhood, feel the safety net of it cocoon and save me. The magic doesn't work any more. Nana leans across the table and hugs me.

'Come on. Tell me what's up. You're acting funny since you got here. It's Jade, isn't it? Ye had a fight. Sure that's nothing new with the pair of ye – ye'll be grand in a few days again.'

'I can't. I don't know ... Nana, I don't know.'

'I'm worried, Saoirse. I think you're gearing up for a turn – a big one. I said it this morning and I stand by it. That therapist fella down there is useless. Marie's friend's sister is great. She's out the Ennis Road – I can get you in to see her? She sorted out Frankie Ward and he was talking to himself and all and seeing God in Aldi.'

I want to be little. For Nana to have collected me from school and me sitting with a bowl of cereal and cartoons and telling Nana all my grievances. The exam I did badly in, the class bully and the mean things she said, the rain, the soccer practice I hated, Eva's constant chatter. The small annoying things that seemed so big. Nana would listen, offer solutions that never worked, make me toast and milky tea. It always made me feel better.

'Is it the debs thing? Don't go if it's upsetting you. You were never a debs kind of girl. Now, Eva's a different story.

She'd be happy going to one every night of the year. I really want us to have a party, though. We need one at this stage.'

'It's ... it's ... I don't know.'

'That place – Cloughmore. I warned your father when he dragged ye off down there and your poor mother not even cold. Sure that place'd depress anyone – middle of nowhere, like. Do you want Weetabix instead of that? I'll get you some and I'll warm the milk for you.'

She gets up and busies herself. I force my brain into lockdown. Revert to a clean sheet. Nana doesn't need to know all the stuff and anyway she can't help me. I know that now. The safety net has been taken away.

'I'm fine, Nana. I'm just over-reacting to everything.'

The Weetabix tastes great. Mushy, warm comfort food.

'You'll be back here in a few weeks, going off out to UL for yourself. I've your room set up – I got you a desk and a fancy reading lamp. You won't know yourself,' she says, patting my hand.

'Thanks.'

'That business with Finn is over, in the past. It's all going to change now, love, onwards and upwards.'

I nod my head and give her a smile. I shouldn't have come here. I can't ever show Nana the black inside me. The 'funny' business in my head. I can't tell her that I'm not normal no matter how many desks she gets me. I can't tell her that I don't want to live here with her where she'll see the real me. The dark, miserable me that makes shit happen to everybody. Nothing gets better. Everything gets worse.

'Sorted?' She's ordering me to be sorted so I nod again.

'Good. Now, we'll tidy up and watch *A Place in the Sun* – I've it recorded,' she says, as she tidies up plates and glasses. 'We might even have a glass of wine. I loves a glass of wine at night.'

We're halfway through *A Place in the Sun* – featuring a couple with a tiny budget and a long list of must-haves – when the doorbell goes. Nana rushes out and Archie Cat gives me filthy looks. I think I'm sitting in his spot. I can hear voices, and then Nana's pushing Jade through the door.

'I'll get them now,' says Nana. 'Sit down there, Jade. Do you want a bowl of stew?'

'No, thanks – I've eaten,' says Jade and sits on the edge of the sofa opposite me, pretending to watch the TV.

'Jade, I –'

'Don't. I'm only here because your nana asked me to call.'

'I just wanted to say ...'

'Sorry? That'd be a first.'

'*You* should be saying sorry.'

'Why?' she asks.

'You came down there with that ... with Nicky and sold drugs to –'

'Oh, for fuck sake. If it wasn't us selling it would be someone else. Nicky's right – you're a spacer, you really are.'

'Thanks.'

'Just being straight, like – and stop pretending you live in a fucking Jane Austen novel. Everyone does molly – like, everyone. Do you think that was Finn's first time? Do you?'

'He didn't ... he wasn't ...'

'Cop on. Do you know how much money he owed Nicky? No? Course you don't. Here's a fucking question – did you actually know him at all?'

Nana arrives back with a bundle of Dulux colour cards. She spreads them out on the coffee table in front of Jade.

'Jade's helping me pick out colours for the kitchen – she's a great eye for colour, haven't you, love?' says Nana. 'I like that one there – Cappuccino Froth or Lemon Curd. Jaysus, you'd get hungry reading these charts. Look at that one – Strawberry Soufflé – the fella who did this chart thought he was doing a menu ...'

Nana's voice trails off as she picks up on the icy silence. Jade shuffles through the cards and the narrator's voice on the TV fails to warm the air. I'm digesting what Jade said and I want to believe she's lying. I know she's not. And she's right. I didn't know Finn at all. None of us did. We knew parts of him – different parts – and still we didn't have the full picture. All of him.

'This one,' says Jade, handing the chart to Nana. 'That'll be perfect in the kitchen.'

She stands up, brushes cat hair from her black jeans and goes to leave.

'Jade ... can we talk?' I say but she's pulling a Megan – I'm talking to her back. She walks out, slamming the front door on the way.

'I thought ye'd sort it out,' Nana says.

'You made it worse,' I say and it's like landing a slap on her face.

'I was trying to fix it, that's all.'

'I'm not six any more. I can look after myself. Nana, just leave me alone, please?'

Nana leaves and I scrunch my eyes tight so that I don't cry. Every single person I touch ends up dying or hating me. I'm not sorted or normal or young or carefree or any of the things I should be. I'd love to close my eyes and never wake up.

18

It feels like it's been raining for weeks – low cloud spitting drizzle on Cloughmore, blanketing us in grey sea mist. Can weather make you tired? All I want to do is sleep and I drag myself out of bed on my day off to meet Dylan. He's back from Spain, more golden, more highlighted – he'd blind you, really. He's working a shift at Lord's Cove and the clouds have finally lifted. I'm walking the prom, scanning the bay for him. I see him out at sea on the rescue paddle board, shooing the local weird dolphin away from swimmers. I watch him stretching down, the dolphin reaching up to touch his hand with her nose, and then he paddles out towards the horizon, arms splashing so she'll follow him.

The others are here. Of course they are. Megan in a bright yellow bikini, all long legs and flicky hair. Cian squashed into swimming trunks he's probably had since he was ten. Kate following Megan like her PA – handing her towels and drinks and sun cream. The Clancy twins, freckles on freckles, red hair gleaming in the bright white light. Eva's here too, her little group stationed a bit away from the others. She's lying on my good red Munster towel – bitch – with Cian Burke's younger brother. They're kissing and it looks strange – my kid sister old enough to kiss lads. He has the same meathead looks as his brother. It makes sense now, Eva and her disgust of me: I bit her boyfriend's brother's ear. Off – if you were to believe the rumours.

I stay on the prom, reluctant to draw attention to myself. Since Limerick and Jade, I've found a way of surviving that I can handle. Work. Sleep. Malcolm when I absolutely have to. Guitar. Books. I'm counting down the days to college and an end to Cloughmore and its tight, tiny world. Dylan's arrival back from Spain has changed that and the stupid fucking sun – you can't be lolling in bed when it's sunny, according to Dad. Dylan's wading back in on the board and he pulls it up at the lifeguard's hut. I'm about to call out to him but stop myself. He makes his way to his pals and they all hug him, even the Clancy twins, like he's just back from an Arctic expedition. Megan pulls him down beside her on the sand, offering him some of her towel. They chat, heads bent together, his arm on her shoulder. They look perfect and in my head I know that this isn't Insta – that they both have shit going on – but there's something about them that's right, that fits. Like a maths equation when the answer looks good. Kate's taking a selfie of the whole group and they're jostling for position and laughing and I need to go home. My stomach's acting up and my heart is a drill in my chest and I can't look away. Megan's swinging out of Dylan and he picks her up and runs towards the shoreline.

She's screaming and laughing. He drops her into the sea and she pretends she's drowning and Dylan, perfect, gorgeous, golden Dylan, saves her. He's running up the beach with her in his arms, her long legs waving in the air. He lays her on the towel and she catches his face with her hands and says something and I wish I could lip read. Now they're sharing a Coke, each taking sips until she grabs the can and downs it all. More laughing and play fighting and fuck this I'm going home.

It's a long walk to Cloughmore. A steady stream of traffic comes towards me, heading for the beach. The sun's hot on my head and my leggings are glued to me. I'll go home, take the guitar down to the far field, bring my book and ice-cold water. I'm halfway home, talking to a grey horse in a nearby field, when my phone vibrates in my pocket. Dylan. I smile at the horse and answer the phone.

'Dylan – sorry – I didn't make it ...'

'Saoirse Considine?'

'Yes?'

'This is Garda Frank Murtagh in Cloughmore Station – there's been a bit of an incident ...'

'Is it my dad? Is he OK?'

'It's your brother. He told us to ring you and wouldn't give us your father's number. Can you come to the station?'

'Of course. I'll be there in, like, ten minutes,' I say.

I run the rest of the way, I run as hard as I can, sweat popping from me, hair lank with it, all the passing beach-goers staring at me. I force my brain into shutdown to avoid Malcolm's catastrophic thinking, but the thoughts find a way in anyway and by the time I reach the station I've decided that Aran has murdered somebody or tried to take his own life or ... or ... I push open the door and run to reception.

'My brother ... Aran Considine ... he's here and ...'

The receptionist gives me the once-over and makes a call. I'm heavy-breathing right into her face so I step away and try to get air into my lungs, which seem way too small for my body.

'Hello – I'm Frank Murtagh. He's down here – follow me.'

I trail the guard, a big, tall, raw-looking fella with a guard's head on him, as Nana would say. He stops outside a door with a glass window and I can see Aran inside, seated at the table, head in his hands, sobbing.

'Here she is, Aran,' says Garda Murtagh. 'Sit yourself down there and Aran'll tell you the story.'

I sit next to Aran and he falls into my arms, muttering and crying and trailing snot everywhere. His backpack is on the table, its contents strewn across it. There's a bundle of boxer shorts, a polaroid of Izzy Goat and a fierce selection of sweets and cakes.

'I'm sorry, Saoirse, I'm sorry. I'll never do it again but don't tell Dad cos he'll be crying and he won't be able to look at me at all and ... don't tell ...'

He launches into another fit of sobbing. I hug him to me.

'It's OK, Ar. It's grand, like,' I say, rubbing his head. 'What happened, Garda Murtagh?'

'Call me Frank. Aran here was caught stealing in SuperValu,' he says, sweeping his hand towards the haul from the backpack. 'He was getting ... ah ... supplies, isn't that right, Aran?'

Aran tries to sob-answer but he's not making sense.

'We got a call from the store detective in SuperValu ...'

'They have a store detective?' I say.

He smiles. 'Look, it's not the stealing he was concerned with – more Aran's reasons.'

Aran's crying is plaintive now. It cuts right into me.

'He was running away. They got worried in SuperValu so they contacted us. And the poor lad thought we were sending him to jail, didn't you, Aran?'

'I'm so sorry – we'll pay for the stuff – my Dad'll –'

'You're grand. I paid for it.'

'Thank you. I'll pay you back,' I say.

'You work in that new place, don't you?'

'I do.'

'Will you ever start doing hot chicken rolls? This town is crying out for them. I went in there once and 'twas pure foreign, the menu. Sure I didn't know what half the stuff was.'

I laugh, too loud and shaky and bonkers. I feel relief but a gnawing anxiety too. Aran's sobs have eased, and I have a web of snot across my chest. Frank pushes a box of tissues towards me.

'I just wanted to make sure the lad was all right and that ye knew what happened. There'll be no charges, Aran. Sure didn't we pay for the stuff in the end?'

He looks again at the array of contents on the table. 'Smart packing too, lad. Seven pairs of boxers. One for every day of the week. Where were you planning on going? You never told us?'

Aran takes a tissue and wipes his face and nose. 'Belfast,' he says, his voice tiny.

'Belfast. That's a long way. Why Belfast?'

'The Titanic Experience. I wanted to see it and ... and ... I saw it on Youtube and ... I wanted to be far away ...'

'Why?' says Frank, his voice gentle.

Aran shrugs. 'Nobody sees me. I'm invisible.'

'We'll have to get you a part in a Marvel film, won't we?'

'I've no friends.'

'You've me. Sure we're best buds now after our adventures today.'

'Nobody talks to me at school and I'm going to secondary school in September and I hate it already and ... Belfast looks nice.'

Frank reaches out and grabs a Snickers, peels off the wrapper and hands it to Aran. 'When I started here, I knew nobody. I hated it, Aran. I'm from way up the country and I'd no friends and sure I was feeling awful sorry for myself, thinking nobody here liked me. And do you know what it was?'

Aran's eating his chocolate, eyes glued to Frank. 'What?'

'See, I was a bit like you. Invisible. And then I copped it – I was making myself invisible. Not talking to the others. Not making an auld effort.'

'What happened?' says Aran.

'I started off small, making a bit of chat about the football or the hurling or that, and sure then I was playing on the five-a-side and I'm flying it now. It took a while, though.'

I'm looking at Frank, at the kindness oozing from his big meaty face and I'm thinking he'd give Malcolm a good run for his money in the therapy stakes. I feel like telling Frank all my problems and worries and then sitting back while he makes them normal and trivial and solvable. He leans over and starts packing Aran's bag, whistling a Marvel theme.

'Now, you're not to be worried about anything, Aran. I'll call out to your dad tomorrow and have a chat with him and you'll be grand, wait and see,' he says.

Outside the station, the sun blinds us and Aran takes a pair of sunglasses from his pocket and puts them on. The tag is still on them: €29.99.

'Where did you get those?' I say, as we cross the road. I know the answer already.

'The pharmacy at the corner – you know the one with the bitchy owner?'

I laugh. 'You can keep them – just this once. You stole the dearest pair in the shop.'

He smiles, stupid head on him with sunglasses falling off him. I hug him and he pushes me away.

'Stop – they'll see.'

'Who?'

'You know – all the lads – and they'll slag me and call me a sissy and a weirdo.'

'Don't mind them, Aran.'

'They know everything.'

'I don't care about them. Gowls.'

My phone buzzes in my pocket. I'm waiting for another shit-show but it's Dylan.

'Where are you?' he says. 'I've been waiting here by myself.'

Liar.

'Something came up. I'm in Cloughmore.'

'I'll come in for you. Meet me at Centra.'

He hangs up before I even have a chance to answer. I consider just going home but decide to go to meet him. Aran is a perfect buffer and there's something annoying me about Dylan, about golden boy Dylan and his efforts to be everything to everyone. But it's even more than that.

19

'Am I on a date with ye? That's, like, really weird,' says Aran as we climb out of Dylan's car.

'We're going to watch the high tide, Aran – highest of the year so far,' says Dylan.

There is sharp salt in the air and the sea is heaving and screaming. The prom's crowded with wave watchers. I look back but there's no Aran. The wind whips my hair as I march back to the car. I bang on the window but he doesn't raise his head. Fuck. I climb back into the car.

'Are you coming?'

He shakes his head. 'I can see them from here.'

'Who? Come on – we'll go to Ruby's after for food.'

'Don't want to. I'm grand here.'

'Aran.' He's crying again. 'What's up?'

He fists tears from his eyes. 'Nothing.'

'Come on, tell me.' I'm watching the waves as they sneak over the wall and drench the spectators. Children scream in delight. Gangs of teens are now standing on the wall, dripping salt water and urging the waves to come. Dylan's being all lifeguardy – telling the younger ones to move back.

'Them,' he says.

'The kids?'

'From school. Them.'

'Fuck them.'

He shakes his head.

'Aran, you have to stop caring what others think.'

I kick myself for the Malcolm-cliché use. I can't do any of this. Mind Aran, convince Dad he's not a selfish git, watch Eva swanning around oblivious to all, new fella every second day. No Jade. Nana cool with me. Dylan and his shiny wholesome persona.

Aran's doing that Dad thing with his face, trying to stretch it so he won't cry.

'Tell me.'

He talks to his feet. 'They don't talk to me. I'm invisible. And see that big lad there? Stretchy Downes? He says he's going to kill me and I don't know why.'

He takes a breath, picks at his nails.

'I know what you mean, Aran.'

'Do you? No, you don't. You can get away from here, from our house. The ceilings are so low they make my head explode. I can't say that because ...'

'Because what?'

'Because Dad. Because everyone's sad all the time and it's my fault. The only one who understands is Eva.'

Lovely. Eva. Eva, who doesn't give a flying fuck about

187

anyone except herself. Eva, whose life hasn't been changed one bit by anything that ever happened in our home.

'Eva?' I say this almost to myself.

'She treats me like normal. I just want normal.'

'How? How does she treat you like normal?'

'She fights with me. Calls me names. Asks me to do things for her. Last night I made her a toasted cheese sandwich. She doesn't hover like you and Dad – she doesn't have a big worried face on her every time she sees me.

I want to say to Aran that Eva doesn't care about anyone but herself, that she's a brat, a bitch, a self-absorbed ditz. I want to say that she'd never be the one sitting in a car on the prom talking to her brother. I want him to be on my side in our sister war. I want to be right and for her to be all the horrible things. I say nothing.

'Come on,' he says. 'Let's see the stupid waves.'

'We'll head towards the small beach,' I say. 'It'll be more fun.'

What I mean is that it'll be quieter and he won't have to pass his school mates. He glares at me. I'm doing it again. Hovering. Worrying. I'm another hoverer in his life. We set off down the prom towards Dylan. Aran hikes himself up on the prom wall, grunting with the effort. He walks the narrow precipice, watching the waves, and I have to warn myself not to say anything. He's going to collide with the other kids. *Please be nice to him, please be nice to him,* I chant in my head. They ignore him – they're too busy with a roller on the horizon. I step out on the road as it thunders to land. It hits the prom wall with a giant crash, drenching everyone. I close my eyes, waiting for Aran to fall off. When I open them I notice that the kids have all linked arms. Even Aran.

* * *

The whole village is in Ruby's after high tide. Most of them sport wet hair and damp clothes. Aran's ordering half the menu. Chips, salad. I can see the top of Megan's head in the booth across from us. She's with a lad from the next town and Dylan's craning his head to see what's going on.

'Sure go on over altogether and sit with them, you'll get a better view,' I say.

He laughs. 'Just want to make sure she's OK,' he says.

'There's Eva. Outside on the terrace with a lad,' says Aran. He digs into his lasagne, shovelling huge fork-loads into his mouth.

'Why didn't you turn up today?' says Dylan, his voice casual.

Aran looks at me but I'm too busy staring at a girl with bright pink hair in the corner of the café. Jade. I can just see the back of Nicky's shiny head.

'Earth to Saoirse?' says Dylan.

Jade's eating a burrito, horsing into it, a hand flying in the air, telling one of her stories. Jade. I have a physical hard pain in my heart. I miss her. More than Finn. I miss her. I'm debating in my head whether to go down and just talk to her and I'm trying to build myself up for it, even though she hasn't answered any of my texts or taken my calls.

'I was in jail and Saoirse had to spring me – like in the movies,' says Aran.

'What are you talking about? Saoirse, what's he on about?' says Dylan. He follows my eyes down to the corner table.

'I was running away and took some stuff from SuperValu and Saoirse sorted it out and Frank – he's a guard – was funny. He's my pal now,' says Aran. 'Can I have ice cream?'

'Eventful day,' says Dylan. 'Sure. Ice cream for the criminal.'

My body's sucking the anxiety from the ether and spitting it back into me, putrid and acrid. I feel locked to the inside seat of this booth in this place. I feel sweat dribbling down my forehead and my lips are dry and salty.

I have to talk to her. I have to. I have to. I can't move. Dylan's talking to me and it takes me all I can do not to slap him. It's the sight of Cian Burke coming towards us that forces my body into action. I jump up from the table, knocking Aran's Coke, and push Dylan out of the way with my legs. I push past Cian, and if I wasn't going to throw up, I'd bite his other fucking ear off. I'm composing what to say in my head, twenty versions of *sorry* and none of them are right. I reach the table and I'm motor-mouthing: *Jade how's it going are you here for long why didn't you call me and* ... and it takes a second for my eyes to catch up with my mouth. The table's empty. Nobody there. It's perfectly set for the next diners, so there's no hint of Jade, ghost or real.

I burst through the emergency exit and run down to the sea wall and hang over it like a drunk. I puke up my dinner in noisy globs. Walkers tut-tut behind me. Acid burns my throat and I cough and splutter the last remnants onto the rocks below. I sit down on the wall, Malcolm-breathing. Fuck. I hate my life. The black fist inside me bursts out and I slap my phone hard on the concrete path. Dylan's walking towards me. He kneels, picks up the phone, slots it back together and tests it.

'Perfect,' he says. '3310. Indestructible.'

'Thanks.' My vocal cords are laced with acid. I feel another wave of vomit fighting its way up my throat. I try to swallow it back down but it wins. I hang over the sea wall again, Dylan holding back my hair while a string of never-ending bile erupts from me. Even when it's gone and my stomach is empty, I continue to dry-heave.

'Sorry,' I say, between the retches.

'It's nothing,' he says. 'Here. Have some water – rinse your mouth out with it.'

I take a slug of water and spit it over the wall. My stomach reacts to more puke fodder and I try to breathe through it.

'Come on,' he says. 'Down here.'

He takes my hand and we walk down the slipway and towards the rocks that frame the beach.

'Sit – come on – you're shaking,' he says. 'It's OK – the tide is on the turn – we won't drown.'

I sit down next to him and for a minute we're silent.

'Aran ...'

'He's fine. Kate's with him and your sister came in when she saw you leaving. Feeling better?'

A huge wave rolls in and almost reaches us. I lean against him and watch as another roller approaches. My body tenses, waiting for it to smash into us. It loses its power just as it hits the rocks.

'I probably ate something dodgy.'

Dylan picks up a round stone, washed smooth from the sea, and skips it over the water. Seagulls screech overhead us and hover over the waves looking for jetsam from the high tide. I want to ask Dylan if he saw Jade too but I'm too scared of the answer. I feel empty and light and want to stay here, leaning against him, anchored, for ever.

August

20

'You promised.'

I open my eyes.

'Dad said to leave you alone but you promised.'

Aran's standing over me, poking me with his finger.

'Ouch – stop, Aran, that hurts.'

'You promised.'

I sit up. Light streams through the window. I can smell toast. And eggs. Always eggs. I pick up the phone and check the time. Nine.

'Fuck. Work. I've got to get dressed.'

'Is it over?'

'What?' I'm out of bed and jumping into a pair of just-washed jeans and a T-shirt.

'Ew,' says Aran, hiding his eyes. 'Is it, though? Over?'

'I don't know what you're talking about. Where's my hairbrush? That bitch Eva ...'

'I'll tell Dad you're better.'

'Wasn't sick.' I find the brush under the bed. Jesus, I look like shit.

'You did it again. You stayed in bed for three days and you promised.'

He glares at me and pounds out of the room, slamming the door. I'm spraying myself with Eva's deodorant and feeling guilty over the ozone layer but am too late to shower.

Dad's in the kitchen, stirring scrambled eggs.

'Saoirse. How are you?'

'Grand. I'm heading into work. I think I had the flu or something.' His face is pinched with worry and I have a mad urge to make everything all right for him. I hug him but it's awkward and overdramatic. It only makes him more worried.

'Results soon,' he says and places eggs and toast on the counter.

'Yeah. I keep forgetting.' I dig into the eggs.

'That lad called a few times but I told him you were ... you had the flu.'

'What lad?'

'Dylan. Nice lad. I know his father from the markets. They're from over Creagh way, aren't they?'

'What did he want?'

'He just asked if you were here. I rang Joey and told him you were sick.'

'Thanks.'

'He left something for you.'

'Joey?'

'Dylan. What did I do with it?'

Dad goes on a hunt, rummaging through egg boxes and piles of basil. Dad's new crop. I pick up a bunch. It smells of Italy, although I've never been. Earth and rain.

'Here.' He hands me a box, wrapped in brown paper with red ribbon. *What the fuck?* I put it on the stool beside me and pour myself tea from the bright orange pot. I love that pot. It's so weird. I'm noticing things like I've been away for months.

'Open it,' says Dad, leaning his arms on the counter. 'I'm dying to know what it is.'

'Later,' I say. I can see the disappointment on his face. I don't want to open it.

'Please? I'm excited for you.'

Aran has wandered into the room and leans next to Dad. Two sets of eager eyes now. I pick up the parcel and shake it. I've no idea why or how this will help determine what's inside. I pick at the red ribbon and Aran's fighting hard not to take the box and rip it open himself. I tear off the brown paper, careful not to rip it too much.

'What is it?' says Aran.

I'm laughing too much to answer him. It's a poker set. A full-on, kick-ass poker set. There's a Post-it note on top:

Debs in 10 days.
Thought this was better than a corsage yoke. X

I drop the note on the counter and Dad picks it up.

'Ten days?' says Dad. 'Why didn't you remind me – there's so much to do. I was going to build a pergola down the field – maybe I still have time.' His eyes light up with the thought of a new project.

'I don't want to go,' I say. 'My idea of the seventh circle of hell.'

Aran picks up the poker set and shakes it. Family trait. Shake gifts.

'Will you teach me, Saoirse? Poker's cool. I play it online sometimes.'

'Online gambling? Is that what you're up to now?' says Dad.

'Only on Saturday night,' says Aran, throwing me a wink. 'Are you going to the debs? Please? A party'd be kind of cool.'

I look at his eager face. Normal. All he wants is normal.

'I'll think about it,' I say.

He jumps around the kitchen, like we'd just won the lotto, and then he and Dad do a happy dance with flicks and kicks and waltzes. I smile at them and stupid tears water my eyes. It's like normal. The normal we had back in Limerick. Aran even looks different. Not pale and haunted. A part of me is grateful to Dylan for bringing laughs back into our house. Another part of me feels like I've signed my contract for the gallows.

'You need a dress! We'll go to Limerick, I'll ring Nana, she'll love all the fuss.' Dad's rooting for his phone and I can feel the snowball of the debs gathering weight and speed.

'Tonight? Promise?' Aran says.

'What am I promising now?' I say.

'Poker. I want to learn to play properly. It's a class set, look.'

It is a class set. Slick silver box, lovely pieces. It must have cost him a few bob. Hours of lifeguarding on a rainy beach. Aran pops bread into the toaster. He's wearing Munster pyjamas that are way too small for him.

'See you later, Aran – for a poker classic.' I grab my bag and head out the door.

'Don't forget,' Aran calls.

Outside, the day is warm and new. Dad's flowers are blooming along the driveway. I can smell their perfume. I saw a movie once where the guy was living in a television show but he didn't know. Today feels like that. Everything is right and on schedule and predictable. The sun shines, the birds sing, I'm going to work in the café. The coffee machine will groan and splutter. Joey'll make super salads and run for surf. I'm whistling as I walk. Just like Dad. I can't think of the name of the movie.

'Saoirse, how are you? Feeling better?' Joey's filling display cases with fresh dishes. Neil Young's whining in the background.

'I'm much better,' I say, as I slip on my apron. The coffee machine looks neglected. There are fingerprints all over it and a dust of coffee grinds. It needs a good scrub.

'Breakfast?'

'I ate at home, Joey.' I begin the cleaning ritual.

'Sure you're OK?'

'Never better. How's the baby?'

'He's so smart, Saoirse. He follows our voices with his eyes. He's smiling already.'

I'm surprised he's not surfing. Joey's going to be one of those parents who thinks their baby is Einstein crossed with Mozart and Marie Curie.

'That's cute.'

'Tea?'

Joey's learning Irish ways fast. Tea. For every occasion. I polish and scrub until the machine is back to its shiny best. The tiny dent from music night annoys me, though. Joey's made a pot of peppermint tea and I sit at the table with him. I'm full of energy. I want to scrub and clean and polish. I want to crank up the coffee machine and hear it groan from overuse. Sunlight streams through the window and flecks the walls with shimmery light. A weekend in bed can be a good thing.

'So, I was thinking we could have another night of music next Friday? It's been over a month.' He sips his tea and beams at me over the rim of his cup.

'Great. Why not?' I say. I'm loving this new me.

'Good. I'll do up the posters tonight.'

There are crumbs on the floor by the window. And jam prints on the wall. I get up and get my gloves.

'Hey – finish your tea, you haven't touched it,' says Joey.

'I'm fine,' I say, spraying the wall with a biodegradable cleaner. 'I'm fine.'

He changes the vinyl record, cutting poor Neil off mid-whine. 'I love this band, Saoirse. Saw them fourteen times. Talking Heads. *Stop Making Sense.*'

I know Talking Heads and am wondering how woke Joey never seems to play female artists. That needs to change.

I halt my scrubbing as the café fills with music. Joey's dancing as he sips his tea. I'm frozen in a wonky movie, my hand still motionless on the wall. Talking Heads. That's what we are.

I'm almost home when I remember Aran and the stupid poker promise. I told him I'd produce Dylan somehow. The day is still perfect. I can smell hay being saved and hot tar from the road. I want this to last. The perfect day. The perfect home. I text Dylan.

> Trying out poker set at mine tonight.
> Call over if you like.

I can do normal. It's easy. The phone beeps a reply straight away:

> Strip poker?

I thumb an answer:

> Sure. My dad'd love to see you naked.

He comes back:

> Hahaha. Will be over in a while.
> Just finishing a shift.

I hate people who write laughs in texts.

OK. See you then when you're done shifting her.

He does it again:

Hahaha.

That was too easy. Things aren't meant to be easy. The chickens screech when they hear me coming and Izzy Goat canters towards me. *The Truman Show*. That's the name of the movie.

21

I'll clatter Eva in a minute. She's nearly sitting on Dylan's lap and what the fuck is she doing with her eyelashes? Has she conjunctivitis? Dad is as bad, coming in and out of the living room like Mrs Doyle, offering tea and scones and bunches of basil for Dylan to take home. I feel outside myself, like I'm watching this scenario on Netflix but unable to fast forward. Aran's loving every minute. Dylan has that effect on people. Makes it all golden. How the fuck does he do it? Be himself but bring everybody onside?

'Look, Dylan, my best poker face,' says Eva. She pulls a pouty Insta pose, all eyes and duck mouth. Dylan laughs and continues dealing cards. I think in my head of ways I could torture Eva. She's all dressed up in a tight green dress, a teen disco special, and her make-up is flawless. It's also two inches thick.

'Are you going to Megan's eighteenth on Saturday night?' she says now.

'Yep, going early so I don't miss any of the fun,' I say. She throws me a withering look.

'I was asking Dylan,' she says, doing her classic eye roll.

'You can tag along if you like – over-eighteens, though,' I say. 'I don't think they want kids there.' That one lands perfectly.

Aran's smiling at his cards. He'll never make a poker player.

'Are you going though, Saoirse?' Dylan says.

I laugh. 'You must be joking.' A thought zaps my brain. It's Finn's birthday too.

'Come with me – it'll be grand,' he says. 'Her mam said to ask you.'

Eva's fiddling with her water bottle but listening to every word.

'No. Don't think so. Not my thing,' I say, hoping he'll drop the subject.

'There's a barbecue on the rocks in Cloughbeg before – it'll be epic,' he says, taking my hand. 'Please?'

There's a gentle knock on the door. Here we go but this time I'm glad of the interruption. Dad arrives in with a tray of Cokes and popcorn.

'I thought ye might be hungry,' he says. He puts the tray on the sideboard and stands there, surveying us. He's beaming.

'We're fine, Dad, just recovering from the scones and biscuits,' I say.

He smiles. Doesn't move. It's like he's outside himself as well, watching this movie, waiting for the happy ending.

I catch Dylan's eye and he winks at me and something in that tiny gesture makes me feel special. A wink is a secret. A small, almost imperceptible hint of intimacy. I like winks. I return one but it's awkward, and beady-eyed Eva notices. Her eyes growl at me. I have a new torture for her. I should have thought of it ages ago. I lean in towards Dylan, resting my elbow on his knee as I choose a card. I can feel Eva tensing. I pick a card and smile at Dylan. He reaches out a hand and puts a stray lock of hair behind my ear. I could kiss him for that. Suck that one up, Eva.

'What's a straight flush again?' says Aran, peering at his hand of cards.

'Aran, the first rule of poker is never ever ask questions,' I say.

'I'm trying to learn, I have to,' he says.

'It's when all your cards have the same suit. Like a hand of clubs or hearts,' says Dylan.

His thigh touches mine and the pressure is lovely. Dad's watching and I try to tell him with my eyes to leave but he's pretending to tidy the bookcase, sneaking glances over his shoulder. Fuck sake. I wish they'd all leave so that I could have a decent shift off Dylan. I'd kind of forgotten how he makes me feel. Eva, the sneaky bitch, is laughing and leaning into Dylan, whispering something to him. I lift my leg and the coffee table rises and flips over on its side. The cards are everywhere.

'Sorry,' I say, 'I'm so clumsy.' Eva's bottle of water has spilled on her dress. There's a dark stain spreading across her stomach. Nice.

'Look what you did!' She stands up, water dripping down her fake-tanned legs.

'It was an accident,' says Dylan.

'It was an accident,' says Dad. 'I'll get a towel.'

'Don't bother, I'll have to change,' says Eva.

I'm holding in the laugh. Aran's not.

'Looks like you peed yourself,' he says. He's cracking up.

Eva flounces out, standing on the cat's tail on her way. Merlin turns panther and tries to lash her legs. Aran's crying laughing now and so am I. Two gone, one to go.

'I know, we'll watch a movie.' Aran's a tough one to get rid of. 'Do you like horrors, Dylan?'

'I do, Aran, but would you mind if we wait a bit? There's, like, something I want to talk to Saoirse about,' says Dylan. The pressure from his thigh has increased.

'Grand,' says Aran. He doesn't move.

'In private,' says Dylan.

'I get it. Smooching time,' says Aran. He picks up Merlin, takes one of Dad's Cokes and leaves.

'I'm sorry, they're all bonkers,' I say.

'No worries,' he says.

I get up, take the coal scuttle and place it against the door. I sit down next to him and I've that stupid tingly feeling in my body again. I love the smell of him. Aftershave and sea.

He fidgets with his hands.

'I know what you want to talk about, Dylan. I'm just not able ... I can't.' There's a rock-hard boulder in my throat.

'I get that. It's just ... his birthday and I'm really missing him and ...'

I pull away from him. Give myself distance. Silence stretches out between us, like a wall.

'Fuck,' he says. 'I'm a disaster.'

'Me too.'

He laughs and leans towards me. We kiss, a proper shift, and I pull him back to me on the couch. His breathing is ragged or is that mine? I slip my hands under his T-shirt and feel warm hard flesh. He's kissing my eyes, nose, my neck. I have that clean-sheet feel in my head again, like we can start over with no Finn between us, no anything. Just two people who like each other. This is easier than talking. More fun too.

I hear a knock on the door. Dad. Fuck. I don't stop kissing him, though. He doesn't stop either, not even when there's a loud rap. His hands are underneath my shirt, touching me with slow strokes. If all my family disappeared right now, I'd drag him up to bed. I can feel them encroaching, though. Hovering.

'Fuckers. Hang on a sec,' I say, crawling out from under him. I straighten my shirt. He runs a hand up my thigh. I go out to the hall, ready to thump Dad.

'What's wrong, Dad?'

And then I hear it. A wailing from upstairs. Banshee level.

'Go up to her, Saoirse. She's very upset,' he says.

'Why? What happened?'

Dad shakes his head. 'No idea. She won't talk to me.'

Aran's standing behind Dad, face tight, eyes shiny with tears.

I climb the creaky steps and push open the bedroom door. Eva's lying face down on her bed, her whole body in spasm from crying. I steal into the room and sit on the edge of the bed.

'Eva.'

'Go away,' she sobs.

'What happened?'

More intense crying. I reach out and touch her back. She's still wearing the tight green dress. She doesn't push my hand away.

'Come on, tell me.'

More sobs.

'It's OK. It'll be OK.' I hate myself for the platitudes.

'It's not. It's not. It's not.'

She screams this at me. Rain has started to beat off the skylight and I can hear Dad's low voice downstairs. Open-plan living – inside and out.

'I promise you, Eva – I've been where you are ...'

'No, you fucking haven't. Rory dumped me and he's with Holly Franklin now, like I'm a piece of shit.'

The sobs start over again and I feel relief that it's just about a lad.

'I want Mam.' Her voice is a whisper.

'I know.'

'It's just too hard – he dumped me because I wouldn't ... you know ... do it with him.'

'Bastard.'

She sits up, rubs her eyes so that her mask of make-up shifts on her face. I want to hug her but I think it might be a step too far. Her phone pings and she jumps on it like it's a bomb she needs to detonate. She reads the message and the sobbing starts again.

'Hey,' I say, reaching out my hand. She pushes it away.

'It's your fault,' she says. 'It's your fault.'

'How?' I say, trying to keep my voice neutral.

'How? You bit his brother's ear off – you cheated on Finn and you cheated on Dylan and ...'

She's screaming this at the top of her lungs and my brain tells me that she's just looking for a target for her hurt but my heart disagrees. I remain passive. It makes her angrier.

'Not even denying it, are you? He thought I was a slut – just like you – that's what he said to me and then he dumps me over text and it's all your fault.'

'Slut? He's the slut, Eva – can't you see that?'

I want to take the words back as soon as they're said.

'Jade's Nicky told me you cheated on Dylan too, in Limerick. Serial cheater – liar and a crazy wan and they think I'm the same – why can't you just be normal? Every good thing that happens to you, you throw it away. You make it ugly. Get out.'

She pushes me in the arm and I stand up, afraid she's going to attack. 'Where did you meet Nicky?' I say. 'Are you doing drugs?'

'I swear, you're an absolute freak. You don't even deny all your cheating and shnakiness and then act like the fucking drug squad?'

'Eva – that's not true. Believe what you like, but –'

'Get out of my room. You're bonkers – get away from me ... Dad? Get her out ...'

I leave, heart thumping, breath squeezed from my too-small lungs. Dad's in the kitchen, pretending to wash up.

'Will I go up to her?' he says.

I shrug and he comes over and hugs me and the smell of him – eggs and chicken shit – is balm and I bury my head in his shoulder. Perfect fit.

'I'll go, love,' he says.

I stand there in the tiny kitchen, gulping air like a landed fish. Aran's in the corner on his iPad even though there is no Wi-Fi in this room. He's taking sneaky peeks at me and I smile at him.

'It's OK, Ar,' I say. 'Just teenage stuff.'

I'm saying it out loud to reassure myself.

Dylan. I'd forgotten about Dylan. I don't want to go back in there, but I do. He's sitting on the couch, his head in his hands. I sit down a bit away from him. The rain has turned to storm. I can hear it flaking the window. I can also hear Dad and Eva talking – plain as day. I flick on the TV for background noise. Dylan looks at me. He heard it all. I can tell by his face. I try to concentrate on the flickering images on the screen but they don't make sense.

'I should go,' he says. 'I've the early shift in the morning.'

'OK.'

He cracks his knuckles. I hate that sound. I want him to go but I want him to stay too and tell me that it's OK.

He cracks his knuckles again and I realise that's his version of volcano stomach.

'I'm sorry,' I say.

'For what?'

'For the mess just there and ... you know.'

'I've to go.' Dylan stands up and walks to the door. 'See you,' he says.

He waits at the door for a second and leaves. I turn off the TV and sit in the silent room with the low ceiling. The rain is heavier now and I strain to hear Dylan's car on the driveway. At last it starts up and headlights fill the dark room. I shiver, though it isn't cold. I struggle in my head to put order on the day. To tidy it, erase bits, highlight other bits. But my head is just questions. *Things I know. I'm a bad person. A shit-magnet. A mess.*

22

We're in Fairy Tail, a boutique in Limerick with a really stupid name. We're all here. Eva came – she can't resist a shopping spree. She's wearing her hitwoman face. Aran and Dad have legged it to Papaz Bistro. It's hell. Eva's being a little strap. She has already had a splodge in Penneys and now she's trying on dresses like she's going to the debs too. I still haven't said anything. I can't find the right moment. And I can't bear the look of disappointment on their faces.

'I'm starving,' says Nana. 'You'd think they'd give you a sandwich or a cup of tea?'

I root in my backpack and find a bag of protein balls that Joey forced on me for the journey. You'd swear they had no food in Limerick.

'Here, Nan, have one of these,' I say, passing the bag to her. She looks at it warily.

'They look like something Izzy Goat'd leave on the ground after a feed of lettuce,' she says, but she takes one anyway. The shop assistant, a tall modelly looking woman with spidery eyelashes, makes a beeline for Nana.

'No food allowed. The dresses,' she says, flashing Nana a smile. She strides away and Nana gives her the finger. Eva's in the dressing room, trying on another dress for a debs that she isn't going to.

'Are you going to try on any?' Nana says.

'I ... it's embarrassing and ... I don't want to go, Nana.'

'Why? That Dylan's a lovely lad, isn't he the fella who helped you when you collapsed?'

I pick my nails, afraid to look at Nana. She is way better than Malcolm at digging and excavating information from me.

'Saoirse, pet, is everything OK?'

I shrug and nod in an effort to disarm the investigation.

'Stay with me tonight, love. We'll watch a film. Have you work tomorrow?'

A shake of the head from me.

'Your dad can pick you up tomorrow night. Least he can do after moving ye to that place. Gives me the shivers every time I go there. I said it to him the last time, I said why can't ye all move back here with me, but no, too proud, like his father, can't admit ...'

Eva arrives out of the dressing room and for once I'm glad to see her. The shop assistant is following like her personal assistant, fixing imaginary folds in a dress that's stunning on my sister. It's full length, shimmery silver. It clings in all the right places and I wouldn't be caught dead in it. It's a dress that screams, *Look at me, I'm gorgeous.* Eva twirls while the shop assistant gushes over her. Nana rolls her eyes at me.

'That's lovely on you, Eva, if you had a debs to go to,' says Nana, 'or the Academy Awards.'

Eva admires herself in the full-length mirror, does a weird bandy model walk across the floor, comes back for another look in the mirror.

'I'm in love,' she says. 'It's, like, perfect on me.'

'It's gorgeous on you, but we're here to get a dress for Saoirse,' says Nan. 'Come on, start trying on a few.'

Nana nudges me. I get up and pick three random dresses from the racks. In the tiny dressing room, I strip with my back to the mirror and pull on the first dress. It's a dusty pink. I hate pink, such a weak colour. I sit on the tiny bench, my clothes in a heap at my feet. I feel like I'm on *Strictly*, and the star of the night has already performed. I hate myself. Every hair, fibre, thought. The whole disgusting package. I walk out, avoiding the many mirrors. They examine me like I'm a dog at a show. Nana's shaking her head. Eva's smirking in her silver swathe of a dress.

'The colour isn't right on you. Try another one,' says the shop assistant.

She's being kind. It's not the colour. It's the package. I want to say it out loud but stop myself just in time. Back in the tiny room, I try on a black dress with beaded bodice and march back out. Fuck it, there is no debs, I'm not going, so it doesn't matter.

'It's ... it's a bit grim,' says Nana.

'You're too pale for it,' says Eva.

The shop assistant looks at me with pity. Eva roots through the racks. She arrives over with a dress, soft teal blue or maybe green. I don't know. She hands me the dress. I take it, like a robot, and return to the hell that is the dressing room. I slip the dress on and catch a glimpse of myself as I walk back out. It fits. It doesn't make me look like a waif. It makes me almost normal.

'That's just beautiful. The colour is lovely on you,' says Nana, leading from the front.

'That's the dress, definitely,' says the shop assistant. She's checking the price tag. 'That's discounted. Half price. It really suits you.'

'We'll take it,' says Nana, beaming at everyone. 'We'll take it.'

Eva's Insta-ing her dress, doing pouty mouth and curvy body. She has sucked her stomach in so much I'm waiting for her to pass out.

*   *   *

I don't stay in Nana's. She'd see right into me. I go home instead, the car silent except for the wipers. I can barely keep my eyes open and I wonder if I have some kind of sleeping sickness or a latent fatal illness that just exhausts you. The further we get from Limerick, the more I think about Mam and how things might be different if she was still here. How she'd know how to fix stuff. Fix me. Aran. Eva. How we'd know where home was again. My brain hurts.

'What did you say?' says Dad, eyes on the slick wet road.

'Nothing.'

'You're talking to yourself, Saoirse,' he says.

Eva snorts in the back seat. 'Nothing new there.'

'Can we stop at Manny's for chips?' Aran says.

'We can't – I've a date, like. I'm late already,' says Eva.

'We'll stop, Aran,' says Dad. 'Sure it'll only take a few minutes – and you better be home by eleven, Eva. It's getting later and later – I'll wait up.'

Eva laughs – she knows Dad'll fall asleep and she can sneak upstairs. I want to say something to her – about being a gowl for lads, about taking that Rory fool back after what she said he did. But I don't have the energy. I'm only thinking now of my bed and sleep.

'Dad – that's the turn,' says Aran. 'You promised we'd get chips.'

Dad swerves the car and we drive down Main Street, quiet at this time of the evening. Timber Hanley's having a chat with himself outside Tully's Bar – a can in one hand and a fag in the other. A man pulls up in a tractor, parks and heads into the pub. A dog sits in a doorway, like he's painted there, and time feels like it's on a loop. Pubs, chippers, work, drunks, pubs. This same dog in the same doorway, every day. My head hurts badly now and I can't remember if I've eaten because time weaves circles around me. Minutes. Hours. Days. Mashed together in a loop. Criss-crossing, repeating, overlapping.

Dad takes food orders and runs in to Manny, who's waving from behind the counter. They're inside. I can see Megan, decked out for the night. Cian Burke's meaty head.

The rust-and-milk-bottle Clancy twins. Kate. Dylan. Finn. The shape of him, his stance, in the corner, reading the notice board. I don't know if this is part of yesterday or today or even tomorrow. I slouch down in my seat, trying to make myself small, and when I look again, the chipper's empty. I can hear tinny music from Eva's ear buds and the beep of a game from Aran's Switch. And another sound, a quiet kind of sobbing. I realise it's coming from me.

23

Things I know. Time can warp and swirl and confuse. My brain feels like it's on fire. I have a pimple over my left eyebrow that looks like Majorca. Things I don't know. How to tell them about the debs. It's three days away and I've played along with the fantasy. I even pretended to have a date with Dylan last night. I have no idea why. I wandered around town, ending up by the graveyard on the stone bench. I felt peace there. A calmness. I like graveyards and dead people. That's another thing I know.

It's music night. Joey's cooking for Munster and I'm hoping he gets the crowds he envisages. Otherwise there will be a glut of hummus and fries and bottled beer.

'Saoirse. Stop. It's polished enough. I can see my face in it.'

Joey's standing beside me and I'm cleaning the coffee machine and I don't even realise I'm doing it. I laugh.

'The crowds will be here soon. At least we're prepared this time,' he says.

'The place looks great – I love the fairy lights.'

'I got them in Ennis – cool, yeah?'

I nod.

'Are you OK, Saoirse?'

'Great. Why?'

'It's just that you seem ... a little off?'

'Off – like bad milk?'

'Not yourself. You fell asleep in the storeroom earlier and I –'

'Time of the month.' A lie but worth it.

'Sure you can do tonight?'

'Yep. Will I open up?' I go to the door before he answers. I flick the sign over and eyeball the street. There are no queues. In fact, there isn't a soul out. It's a dusky late summer evening, streaky pink sky and the smell of September in the air. The dog who lives in the porch across the road spots me and barks. Little shit – I gave him biscuits yesterday. Was it yesterday?

Inside, Joey's testing the amp. He's strumming his guitar, a battered affair that has seen too many surf trips. I take up mine and sit at a table. We fall into a kind of duet and it's lonely and gorgeous. This is what I'd like to do tonight. Strum and mess around with Joey. Play some music. Meet nobody.

The first patrons arrive, a stag party by the looks of them. They're loud and drunk and wearing pink T-shirts that say *Stag Wars* across the front. They order food, and Joey and I get to work. He's put on a Springsteen album while we serve them. I can barely hear Bruce's voice over the noise. But they're buying food and drink and Joey's smiling. He gives me the nod to go up on stage. I'm nervous, like there's

219

something nasty in the room. Something unpredictable and weird. I tune my guitar and the wolf whistles start. I ignore them, concentrate on a spot at the back of the room, where Joey thumped a persistent fly earlier, and sing. They seem to enjoy it and give me a half-civilised clap at the end. I continue, ignoring requests from the floor for Metallica and The Prodigy. I launch into a Beatles medley. They're singing along, waving their bottles in the air and sending beer arcs across the floor. More people have arrived, older couples. Bingo must be over. I finish my set and walk through the crowded tables towards the counter. I feel cold wet hands between my legs as I pass, a swift, almost indiscernible grope, and I'm so shocked, I don't react. I take cover behind the counter, my breaths big gasps of air. I watch the lads laugh amongst themselves and I know which one did it. Balding shaved head, neck fat, swallow tattoo on his arm. They're back-slapping him like he did something brave or good.

I serve the new customers, smile at them, make small talk. Anger and disgust gnaw at me. Disgust at myself for allowing it to happen. For putting myself in line for it to even happen. He comes up to order more beers and I serve him like the stupid obedient female that I am. I touch his money that has touched his hand. He leaves a five-euro tip on the counter. I want to ask him if that's all the feel is worth. I say nothing. I think I smile at him and say thanks. Joey's finishing up. I fill up a pint glass with water and walk towards the stage. As I pass the table I tip the water over Neck Fat, from his head right down to his crotch.

'I'm so sorry,' I say.

'Fuck sake, you stupid bitch,' he says, standing up.

He's drenched. Hair. Stag T-shirt. Jeans.

I smile at him. 'Apologies, simple accident.'

'Get me a towel, you thick bitch,' he says.

'Out, please leave,' Joey says.

'What? She just dumped water all over me and you're throwing *us* out?' Neck Fat is losing his shit.

'Not "us" – just you. Nobody speaks to a colleague of mine like that,' says Joey.

They slug back beers and bang bottles on tables. But they leave.

'I'm sorry, Joey,' I say, as we clean the tables. More customers have come in and are waiting to be seated.

'I didn't like the vibe of them – or the cat-calling when you were singing. No worries, Saoirse.'

I sing another set, but I'm not in the room. I'm at home in bed with Netflix and no people. I close with 'The Seduction of Eve', by a Limerick singer-songwriter called Emma Langford. A singer who makes me choke with envy. It's the perfect song for a shit night and I get lost in the words. I finish and see Dylan and his friends at the back of the room. No Megan. I feel his eyes on me as I make my way back to the counter. I busy myself, counting down the minutes until we can close. I go out to the storeroom and, as I pass, the Clancy twins duck out of the way, pretending to be scared of me.

I slide down onto the floor, heart competing with my breaths for speed and loudness. I hang my head between my legs, sucking thin air. I get that sense again that I've

221

lived this already, that I'm in a permanent *déjà vu* and it's like tinnitus – a constant irritating brain loop. Noise drifts in, high voices, bottles banging, shouts, laughing. I can't get up. It's like everything is sucked out of me. Breath, heart, hope.

'Saoirse? May I come in?'

'Yes.'

Joey sits down beside me. 'You OK?'

I shake my head.

'What's up? Actually – erase that. You don't know, right? It's not any one thing.'

I nod.

'I understand.'

'Thank you,' I say.

'I also have no solutions.'

'Thank you.'

Joey laughs. 'That's what I hate the most when you're going through a shit time. Other people thinking they can shake the life hacks drawer and fix your life. Bullshit.'

'Or tell you to breathe,' I say.

'That too. Look – you don't have to come back out. I'll tidy up. There's just a handful left – probably cleaning the place out as we speak.'

'I'll come.'

'Sure?'

'Sure.'

He offers me his hand and pulls me up.

The place has emptied bar a few stragglers. And Dylan. He's sitting at a table alone, a collection of beer bottles in front of him. Joey and I begin the clean-up. There are sweet potato chips mashed into the floor and somebody played frisbee with the halloumi.

'Saoirse.' Dylan's waving me over. I ignore him. There's something about the way he's calling me, like summoning. It reminds me of the grope.

'Saoirse.' He's behind me. I can smell beer breath. I clear the table in front of me, dumping rubbish into biodegradable bags. He catches my arm.

'Don't touch me.'

'Jesus. What's up? I just want to talk.'

'Talk away. Just don't touch me.'

'Will you sit with me?' he says.

'I'm working.'

'Please?'

I sit at the half-cleaned table. He sits opposite me, beer in hand.

'I ... just ... I ...'

'It's fine. I don't want to go to the debs anyway. Are you done?'

'Fuck it, you're hard work, do you know that?'

'Are you done?' I ask again.

'No, I'm not. Why are you blanking me? I've texted ...'

'Obligatory text.'

'What are you on about? Look – you refuse to talk about ... about our history ...'

I laugh. 'Is that what they call cheating now? That's what we did, Dylan, you and me. We cheated on him. We cheated on Finn. That's our history.'

'Oh, for fuck sake.' His voice is drunk-loud and Joey looks over. I give him the thumbs up.

Dylan pulls his chair closer to mine.

'Saoirse, talk to me. Please. Can we just talk? Do I have to spell it out?'

His voice is sing-song drunk. He's a stag man too, pretends he isn't but he is.

'Spell it out.'

'I thought we were ... you know ... we had something.'

'So?'

'What's going on with you, Saoirse? Why can't you be ...'

'Normal?'

He shakes his head. Slugs more beer.

I laugh. 'You're here all saintly and perfect and I'm the one being ripped apart?'

He's cracking his knuckles. Good. I'm getting to him.

'Same with the debs. My dad's having a fucking debs party. Did you know that? He bought me a dress that he can't really afford and I haven't the guts to tell him that ... that you're another waster. Like everybody in this stupid, backward town.'

He makes eye contact and I think I've gone too far and I don't care. I hear Malcolm's know-all voice in my head saying, *Self-sabotage, Saoirse.* I ignore it.

'Yeah, so you're no saint,' I say. 'You wouldn't know how to be straight if you had a plank inserted into you, so quit with the lectures. I think we're done.'

'No, we're not done. I never fucking claimed to be a saint – that's the last thing I am ...'

Spit flies from his mouth, but he's losing momentum. Getting glassy-eyed. He shrugs and slugs the rest of his beer. I reach for an open bottle and take a huge slug. It's like a shot of adrenalin.

'What's really up with you, Saoirse?'

Jesus, what does it take to beat this guy down?

'My dad's outside.'

'When?' he says. 'Name one time I wasn't straight with you?'

'We need to close up. Joey's waiting to go home and I'm tired.' I fight back stupid tears, rapid-blink so they'll disappear. I can't look at him or I'll melt into him and he'll see. He'll see the sad inside me.

'Hey,' he says, touching my face and wiping away the one tear that survived. 'Hey, come on, it's not all bad.'

I can't answer because there's a pity rock in my throat. I'm so tired. Of all of it. His hand is gentle and smells of beer. He rests both hands on my shoulders and pulls me towards him.

'It's OK,' he says. 'It's grand.'

The tears come back and I try to make them silent. I feel his armour close to me. Normal, hopeful, shiny armour that I'm drawn to but feel I must repel at the same time. Curve balls always come back. Sometimes it doesn't get better, it gets worse. Does he ever feel like this? I take another slug of beer. It's like a belt of energy. I feel like I'm in another movie, one that has no name yet. Did I have this exact conversation before?

'Have you heard of the multiverse?' I say. 'It's like

many realms or universes which sit side by side in higher dimensions and our senses can't perceive them directly. Alternative universes, I guess.'

He shakes his head. Cracks his knuckles.

'This is one explanation for the cold spot – you know what that is?'

Another head-shake.

'The Big Bang – the huge event that gave us the universe, like, billions of years ago – well, it has left its mark on everything we know today. The most permanent, though, is its afterglow. Brain fried?'

He sips his beer. Half-smiles at me.

'Yeah, so this afterglow is the cold spot – a kind of super void – there are controversial claims that this could be a parallel universe, caused by quantum entanglement between universes before they were separated by cosmic inflation – seriously – like this cold spot – its existence – has been confirmed by NASA ...'

He's crying. Soft, tiny sobs into his beer. I've fried his brain.

'I like the parallel-universe theory. Do you ever have days that seem familiar – like you've lived them before? You know – like a continuous *déjà vu* and you know what the conversations will be and sometimes you see ghosts and maybe you don't see ghosts. It's blip-in-time stuff and the conversations you have with ghosts are real but warped in time and space and ...'

He reaches out, takes my hand, head low.

'You should read up on quantum mechanics, Dylan.'

'Naw, I'm grand.'

'Fascinating. Everett, Hawking, incredible minds. Hawking's last scientific paper before he died is kind of about the multiverse. It's called "A Smooth Exit from Eternal Inflation".'

'Light reading, so.'

'I think the work aims to transform the idea of the multiverse in a scientific framework that – wait for it – can be tested. Brain fried yet?'

He smiles. There are tears caught in his eyelashes.

'Can your brain be inflamed?' I often think about that. 'You know – like your body or your leg or your lungs? I think it can, the brain is an organ, like.'

He mumbles something. Leans into me. I'm on a rant, a motormouth of vomited information. Beer should be illegal. Or maybe my brain should be. I can't stop.

'I mean your thought process, what makes you *you*, not the organ, more like the essence of a person.'

He shrugs. 'I don't know any of this stuff, Saoirse.'

'I mean your essence, your mind. Can your mind be inflamed?'

'Why?'

'Mine is. And it hurts.'

He hugs me.

'I told my mother when I was eight that God didn't exist. I'd done the maths, you see. I had a bit of an episode. Mam said I was thinking too hard. Mind overload – like a computer with a full hard drive.'

He pulls away, strokes my face, my chin, my mouth.

'My mam taught me a trick,' I say. 'She said to think of soothing words and chant them.'

'Did it work?'

'I couldn't think of soothing words. She thought of some but they weren't soothing – they made me think too much.'

'Like what words?'

'Oh, you know, things she thought an eight-year-old would like – kittens and ponies and rainbows. And then I found other words and they worked for years before they stopped.' I look at him but he's picking his nails.

'What were the words?'

I've never told any of this stuff to anyone before. I never said it aloud.

'Collective nouns.'

'What?' he says. 'What are you talking about?'

'I love collective nouns. A walk of snipe. A covey of quail. A paddling of ducks.'

'Jesus.'

'A kindle of kittens. A leap of leopards. A deceit of lapwings. An exaltation of larks. They're like poetry. There are fish ones too.'

'Of course there are.'

'A bind of salmon. A company of angelfish. A glint of goldfish. Collective nouns are cool.'

A loud rap at the window makes us jump apart. Dad.

'I'll collect you at seven on Thursday.'

'For what?'

He smiles and sighs. 'The debs. We're going – you're going. It's closure – more than that.'

'I –'

'Saoirse, we're going – together.'

He takes out his phone, drops it and it skitters across the floor. He looks at me, drunken stupid Dylan, and grins. 'I'm a gowl,' he says.

I nod and pick up the phone. I'm afraid he will face-plant if he tries to do it.

'Will you come with me, with this gowl?' He reaches out and touches my hand.

I nod. 'OK.'

Dad's tapping at the window again and Joey's jiggling his keys.

'Good luck on Wednesday, Saoirse,' Dylan says, while pretending he's not swaying.

'Why?'

'Results.' He has the hiccups and he holds in his breath to stop them. It makes them worse.

'Oh. Right. Same to you.'

I want to fall back into him, kiss him and laugh and be the way we were in that pub. It seems like years ago. I turn away to find my phone and cardigan. When I look up, he's gone.

I'm quiet on the way home. Dad gives me my space. We pull into the driveway and he hugs me to him, kisses the top of my head.

'You missed your appointment with your counsellor,' he says into my hair.

'Forgot.'

He hugs me tighter. 'Nana's worried.'

'Why?'

'She says you weren't yourself in Limerick.'

'I was tired.'

'It's OK, Saoirse.'

He pulls me in for another hug and gets out of the car. His shoulders are hunched as he struggles with the keys. He never knows the right key for the front door. Finn's face floats in front of me. Eerie. See-through. Smiling. *A business of ferrets. A siege of herons. A shiver of sharks. A squad of squid. A nest of rabbits.*

24

Results yesterday. Five hundred and eighty points. Who cares? This is not the sum of me. This is just a barometer of my excellent regurgitation skills. I text nobody. I don't go for celebratory drinks with my cool bunch of friends or go to Ruby's after collecting the results from the school. No. I just go online and see the results. I tell Merlin first, but he's unimpressed and continues to lick his butt. Stupid exam anyway. *Things I know. Nothing.*

Nana arrived last night, all business about the party. She brought so much food, we all wondered how she fit it in her Fiesta. And she brought me a gift. A brand-new phone. It's still sitting in its box on my bed. I can smell the newness off it. Nana says it's 'state of the art but not an iPhone because I'd have had to remortgage the house and it's not locked or maybe it is I can't remember, love, there you go.'

My dress is hanging on the back of the door and I don't want to leave the house. That's why I'm sitting at the dressing table, in my knickers and bra, hair wet, face bare and pale. I'm hollow. Empty. Tired. I can hear Nana and Aran downstairs, in full party mode. My stomach is a cacophony of noise. The volcano is bubbling. Merlin's stretched on my bed behind me, oblivious to stress fests. I grab my phone.

Sick. Can't make it. Sorry.

My finger hovers over the SEND button. I hear Aran's laugh, a real belly laugh, floating up the stairs to me. I delete the text. I pull the new phone from the bag and free it from its box. It feels dangerous, not simple and familiar like the old, battered Nokia. I reach over to my locker and search for the broken phone. There it is. I slip out the SIM card and stare at it, small and deadly in my hand. Old WhatsApp messages, voice notes. From Finn. From Mam. From Jade. Photos, memories, time stamps, lives. I slip the SIM into the back of the phone and watch it come to life in my hand. I click into Finn's WhatsApp. A row of voice notes. I drop the phone on the bed, pushing it away with my hand. Fuck. I stretch and pick it up again. I listen, last one first – like that will change the outcome.

27 May 8.10 a.m.
Hi Saoirse, me again. Can you ring me on this?

I can't do this. His voice. I can hear it in his voice, a tiny shake. His last words to me. Ever.

27 May. 8.05 a.m.
*Seesh, I'm sorry… don't… you know… I'm good. Really.
I'm good.*

I drop the phone on the floor. Seesh. His name for me.
Seesh. His last words. I'm shivering and Merlin's spooked
and scratching to get out. I open the door for him and he
skitters down the stairs. The phone is a magnet, pulling
me back towards it, forcing me to pick it up, to press PLAY.

27 May 1.08 a.m.
*Seesh forget the other message. Just delete it, like, it's me
being a dick and you're the best and I don't blame Dylan
at all, like. Or you. It's me, not you haha. I'm good. Sorted.*

27 May 12.33 a.m.
Seesh? Fuck…

There's a tap on the door and the phone clatters to the floor.
   'Saoirse?'
   I'm staring at myself in the mirror, debs dress hanging on
the wardrobe as a backdrop. A tiny stab of pain has erupted
in my head – right behind my eyes.
   'It's me, it's Jade.'
   The door creaks open and she's a colour palette of energy.
Her hair is spiked and blood red. Eye-shadow is red and pink
and orange. Dark brown eyes are her own. She's wearing her
tulle skirt over leggings and Docs and she looks debs-ready
just the way she is.

She eases herself onto the bed beside me, her arm touching mine.

'Big day, huh?' she says to my image in the mirror.

'I don't want to go,' I say.

'Don't, then. We'll get pissed and go laugh at them all later.'

Her arm snakes around my shoulder and I'm hugging her so tight it even hurts me.

'You were right, Saoirse – Nicky was a gowl.'

I pull away. 'You dumped him?'

'Finally. Got me some sweet revenge too.'

'What did you do? I don't know if I want to hear.'

'Got him busted. Really simple, like – he's got a nice rap charge now.'

'Seriously?'

'Yep. I got the bus here, fucking hell, it stops in the most random places, like a tour of rural Ireland and a gowl with a curry – imagine, a curry on a bus – sat next to me. I nearly puked into my shoe.'

I laugh and push the phone under the bed with my foot.

'Jaysus, there's some spread below – your nan's feeding the whole of Clare and, PSA, she's two or three gins in.'

'Are you staying?'

'If you'll have me.'

'Always.'

'Oh my God, is that your dress? I love it, fucking mega. You should go – get dressed up, get pissed and fuck everyone. Oh, and my points? They're shit. I don't need to know yours – they all told me downstairs – brainbox, like.'

'None of it matters, Jade.'

'Well, it does when the only course you can qualify for is equine science. I don't know a horse's face from his arse.'

I'm cracking up. Jade is medicine. There should be a prescription for her.

'Decision time – are you going?'

'Yeah, but will you be on standby?'

'Of course. I'll be dying to hear all the sca. Come on, start putting on the slap.'

I can hear Nana downstairs calling Jade.

'She has forty jobs for me – I'll be back to check on you.'

She leaves and the room feels deflated. I pick up the phone and hover over the last message. Delete. Delete. I press PLAY.

26 May 23.02 p.m.
Saoirse. Dylan told me. Everything. Jesus. I don't want to but I feel bad. He asked me was it ok for him ... to ... you know ... be with you ... and like the answer to that is yours to give. Not me. Am ... I'm raging ... going to be straight with you ... that ye ... you know ... while we ... anyway ring me. I want to talk to you and ... in a weird way I don't blame you ... I'm an eejit ... useless.

My hands are shaking and I put the phone down on the bed. Dylan. Absolute gowl. Selfish bastard. Malcolm-breaths. Deep ones.

I look at the make-up spread across the table. *Prepare a face to meet the faces that you meet.* I lather on foundation. Orange. Awful on my blotchy white skin. Some eye-shadow.

Any colour. Who fucking cares? Mascara. Clumps of black muck coating my eyelashes. Done. I look like an imposter.

Eva comes into the room, sits on the bed with Merlin. I wish she'd leave. It's like the Leaving Cert again but about make-up and its correct application. She watches me. I can see her in the mirror.

'You haven't a clue,' she says, stroking the cat.

'Did you come up here to laugh?'

'No. I came to help. Where are the wipes?'

She's up and over and scrubbing the shit off my face.

'There. Now turn your back to the mirror.'

I obey. I don't know what else to do.

'You need a base first, then the foundation and fixer and contouring.'

She gets to work and I want to tell her to take it easy with the layers, that I don't want to end up unrecognisable like her and her friends. Fuck it. I need a mask tonight.

'Tilt your chin up – that's it.'

Her hands are gentle, almost artistic.

'Thanks. I hadn't a clue what I was doing.'

'Obviously. I can't let you go out like a clown.'

She's concentrating hard, face screwed up as she examines her work.

'I don't want to go.'

She stops, looks at me. 'You have to go.'

'Why?'

She starts applying more shit to my face, rubbing and adding and brushing. Merlin yawns on the bed and begins to groom himself too.

'You have to show them you don't give a fuck.'

'I do give a fuck. Many fucks. I'm not like them. I'm different. Weird.'

'You're not weird. In a city you wouldn't be weird. It's just this place. The rules here, like.'

'What do you mean?'

'Just that you've to be a certain thing and you can't be anything else. I'll do your hair too. Up style?'

'Yeah.'

Eva knows. She knows about turning yourself into other people.

'I'm sorry.'

'Not doing anything tonight anyway. You're grand.'

She's holding the hairdryer like a gun, hand outstretched to switch it on. She blasts my hair with the dryer, pushes my head down to get to the back.

'Ouch.'

'You're grand. There. I want it a bit damp so I can style it.'

She sprays something evil around my head until I gag.

'Jesus. What's that? Pesticide?' I'm coughing my guts up.

'Hairspray. Cop on.'

She checks her armour for more product to dump on my hair.

'I need clips. Hang on – there's some in that drawer.'

She bends over and pulls out a pack of clips. She slips them from the card and piles them in front of her like poker chips. She picks up a brush and backcombs my hair.

'You're full of split ends. You need a trim.'

She examines my hair and pulls curls loose at the front. 'Nice. Suits you.'

Eva switches on the hair dryer, points it at my head. Her hands coax and stroke my hair. It feels good.

'I had to get here before Jade – Nana kept her busy while I came up. You'd be going to the debs like someone from Metallica.'

'Eva.'

'Yeah?'

'Thanks.'

She shrugs. 'You look lovely.'

I'm dressed, hair up, Eva's jewellery on, and I still haven't seen myself in the mirror. She's making final adjustments to the clips. My head's fizzing with voice notes. With his voice.

'You're good to go,' she says. 'Dylan's below. I heard him pull up. Go on – look in the mirror – the full-length one on the door.'

I turn around and see a stranger looking back at me. The make-up is subtle by Eva standards. I look grand. Not like myself, which suits me for tonight.

'Thanks so much, Eva. You did a great job.'

'Welcome. There's something you can do for me.'

'Anything.'

'You know that vintage dress you got in London?'

'Yes.' I'm praying she doesn't ask for a loan of it.

'Can I, like, have it?'

I smile. Typical Eva. Go the whole hog and ask to own it.

'Yep.'

'Go down. They're all waiting.'

We almost hug but somehow step around each other. I teeter downstairs in Eva's heels.

'Bring flats in your bag,' she says. 'Actually, my bag – you only have that gross backpack. And buy your naggins of vodka in the offy before you go in – they'll search you in the hotel so slip it into your knickers or your bra.'

25

They're in the kitchen and they all stare when they see me.

'Is it you?' says Aran.

'I think so,' I say.

'Way to go, our Saoirse. Up the Parish!' says Jade.

'Just stunning,' says Nan. 'You're stunning.'

'Eva's magic,' I say. 'Can I have a drink?'

Nobody moves. They're still staring.

'Wow – this is like a transformation you'd see on the telly,' says Jade.

'Here,' says Dad, putting a glass of something bubbly into my hand. I shouldn't drink it because my stomach is dodgy. I slug it back in one go. Nan's flitting about now with plates of nibbly things. Aran's helping himself to all the food while gluing himself to Dylan's side. Somebody left the door open and Izzy Goat's eating vegan sausage rolls from a plate on the table.

'You look gorgeous,' Dylan says.

I turn to face him. He looks gorgeous himself, suited up and buttonholed. Gorgeous – for a snake.

'I got you this,' he says. 'Your corsage. I didn't know the colour of your dress so I kind of went neutral.'

'It's lovely,' I say, putting it down on the table.

'You put it on your wrist, you eejit,' says Eva. She whips the pale creamy flower from its package and slips it on me. It makes me think of Mam. My head hurts. I don't know if it's the clips or the stress. And you can't delete voice notes once you listen to them. They're playing on a loop in my head.

'We should go soon,' says Dylan.

'Yeah. We might miss something,' I say. I smile to soften the dig.

'Nana wants to say a few words,' says Aran. 'I tried to talk her out of it.'

Oh Jesus. Gin-drunk Nana. Eva has placed a shawl thing over my shoulders and pushes a silver clutch bag into my hands. Nana's gearing up. She's tapping her extra-large gin glass.

'I just want to say a few words,' she says.

'We know, Nan,' says Aran.

'Saoirse is a wonderful girl. We love her to the moon and back, don't we?'

'Get on with it, Nan,' I say.

'She's had her troubles ...'

'Nan, please ...'

'It's been a tough few years but she'll shine. She's sensitive and caring and ... just lovely.'

'Thanks, Nan, we've to go,' I say before she gets dramatic. I push Dylan out towards the hallway.

'Wait, there's way more ...' says Nana but we're already outside. As we pull away, I watch them all in the doorway. They're waving and calling after us. Izzy Goat's head's poking through Dad's legs, Aran's beaming and Nana's still giving her speech. Her few words. Jade's downing a can of Scrumpy Jack. It's a happy image. It makes me feel sad.

'I got drinks – we'll have to stash them going in,' says Dylan. 'I'm leaving the car in the hotel carpark overnight, so no worries.'

I watch the road whip by in a blur of greens. Dylan's talking but he sounds distorted. Under water. As we take the bend to the main street, I look up at the graveyard on the hill. I imagine all the dead people, gathered in groups, watching over their town. Laughing at us poor eejits still here, thinking we're important. To them we're like ants.

We turn in to the tree-lined driveway of the hotel. It hulks over the water, ominous and dark. They've strung fairy lights across the portico but it still looks like the entrance to hell. My headache is black pain now and I'm sweating through the fine gauze of the dress. He parks the car and shoves naggins into his pockets. He roots in the dash and pulls out two red armbands.

'Here, put that on. We're all wearing one – for Finn.'

He pulls his on and waits while I stare at mine. I put it back in the dash.

'Why won't –?'

'Performative shit. I don't do that.' There's an edge to my voice that I know he picks up on.

'Ready?' he says.

Knots of young people make their way through the doors, all in their finery. Groups hug and kiss and screech. It echoes through the evening. It's golden hour and I think of Dad and his little sunset seat.

'Saoirse? Ready?'

Dylan has the passenger door open and I'm rigid in the seat like I'm superglued to it.

'No.'

He runs a hand through his hair and squats on his hunkers, clinking naggins as he does so. 'We don't have to go,' he says.

I'm staring ahead. I want to go home.

'Don't be stupid. I'm ready,' I say, climbing out of the car.

We walk up the driveway, my heels crunching on the pebbles. We climb the steps and I can hear the pulse in my head pumping pain to body parts.

'Let's do this,' he says, kissing me on the lips.

I feel like I've died and am watching my body continue without me. I don't know who I am. I just don't know.

26

I make straight for the bathroom. I leave Dylan in the foyer and run, past the lion statues, past the drinks tables. Inside, I make for a cubicle, pushing a knot of people out of the way. I sit on the toilet and Malcolm-breathe. My phone beeps in my bag. It's Eva.

> Nurofen Plus in zip pocket.
> Get langers and fuck em all but don't bite.

My eyes water at that stupid text. I blink a few times and find the tablets. I dry-swallow two. Eva. She's way smarter than me. I wait until the cackling outside stops before I go out. Dylan's surrounded by them and they're doing their stupid football circle thing and it looks worse now with the armbands. I hover in the stupid high heels. Megan's linking him now, giggling up at him. They are the perfect couple. They match. My hands are shaking and I fiddle with my bag for something to do.

'Saoirse,' Dylan says and beckons me.

My legs shake as I walk over.

'Hi, Saoirse, you look gorgeous,' Kate says.

Cian Burke snorts and the Clancy twins join in, like they've just been given permission. I'm looking at Megan for her reaction. Her acceptance and approval. She looks through me and then walks away.

'Thanks, Kate, so do you,' I say. My voice doesn't belong to me. It's high and shaky.

The others follow Megan, all except Kate. Dylan's taking slugs from a Fanta bottle that isn't Fanta.

'Want some?' he says, offering it to me.

I gulp back the liquid. Vodka. Disgusting.

'Let's go in,' says Kate. 'They're serving the meal.'

'The swill, more like,' says Dylan.

The function room is dark and music from a DJ thumps through the air.

'Over here,' says Kate, winding herself through the tables.

Sweat slides around my face. I can feel my make-up mask melting. Dylan reaches the table first and sits at the only space available – there are two seats right next to Megan and her date, a lad from Ennis. I've seen him before with the group. I know by the cut of him that he drinks too much and sweats testosterone. She's whispering into his ear. I sit next to Dylan. They've served the soup already. No menus or choices here. It's grey slop, so thick I can almost stand my spoon in it. It tastes vaguely of mushroom. Voices soar and laugh around me. I play with my soup, break the dry bread roll, pretend to eat. Megan is in deep conversation with Dylan.

Main course. The vegetarian choice is everything except the meat and gravy. I drink the vodka in my water glass. Every so often Dylan asks if I am OK, tries to make conversation. Megan always interrupts. Shows him something on her phone, asks him a question. Her date is langers at this stage. He'll be asleep soon. Kate is at the other end of the table, killed from smiling down at me. Cian Burke's head is hidden behind the plastic flower centrepiece – the only good thing that has happened so far. The DJ has opted for soft music during the meal. Ed Sheeran shit. Megan's date's singing along to it. My stomach's a burning volcano. Dylan's talking but he's under water again. Fish talk. I nod and smile and wish the night away. This is hell. Every long minute.

The dancing is worse than the food. I don't get dancing. It makes me feel awkward and dumb, moving my body to music I hate. Dylan's drunk-dancing on the floor with Kate, and Megan has managed to put a few tables between me and her. My stomach is churning, the worst it's ever been, bloated and noisy. Dylan comes back, leans in for a kiss. I need the bathroom again – and fast.

'Need air, I'll be back in a sec,' I say, running out towards the bathrooms. I burst into a cubicle and manage to pull my dress up and sit on the toilet before the Mount Etna unleashes itself. I feel weak and sick and press my head on the cold toilet wall. I make a few false finishes before it finally ends. My breath is raspy and loud and I lean my head between my legs, trying not to get my snot and make-up on the dress. A gaggle of screaming women enters just as I'm opening the cubicle door. I bolt it closed and sit on the loo, hoping they won't smell recent events.

I hear a girl's voice as they fix their faces.

'She's a bit odd. I'm a tiny bit scared of her to be honest,' says the voice.

'Can I borrow your lippy?' It's Megan. 'Thanks, I love the colour. Fuck off, Ella, she's nuts. I'm terrified of her. What the fuck is Dylan doing with that one?'

'She's unhinged. I said it from the first day she came to our school. She just latched onto you to get to Finn.'

'And no armband? Has to always be different. I've no idea what lads see in her. I mean Dylan's hot, like,' says the Ella one.

I'm biting my hand so I won't scream at them. Biting down as hard as I can. I wish Jade was here, sucking the energy from them and turning it into humour.

'If she'd never come here, he'd be alive – Finn'd be here with us tonight,' says Megan, her voice teary.

'Aw, Megs. He'd want you to have fun. Don't let her ruin your night – fuck her, I'm just, like, sitting a mile away so she doesn't bite my ear off.'

They laugh, all of them. I push open the door, head high. I can hear gasps, and their eyes are round with fear.

'Look at this – a coven of bitches – or is it witches? Either will do,' I say, my voice steadier than my brain.

'Come on, girls ...' says Megan.

'Have a great night,' I say, walking out. I try to slam the door but it's one of those stupid slow-closing ones. I go in search of Dylan. My bravery has melted and the headache won't budge and Finn's voice notes spin in my brain and I need to go home. I watch faces as I pass tables and I see it now. Some of them laugh and whisper behind their hands. I feel like every pair of eyes in the room is trained in my direction. I take my bag and wrap thing and head out towards the door. I can't find Dylan but I have to get out. I have to. And I have to talk to him first.

I'm on the steps of the hotel when I see them. They're over by the love tree, Dylan holding up a crying Cian. A donkey roars in a nearby field and the moon slides in and out of the clouds. I can hear the river. The rush of water mimics the noise in my head. I keep watching, allowing the hurt to find a home inside me. Dylan sees me but stays with Cian. I walk over as Cian slides to the ground, sobbing his heart out.

'Sorry, Saoirse – he's really upset about Finn. He thinks he pushed him that night by the river – teasing him with the guitar. I'll be back in a minute –'

'I listened.'

He looks at me, puzzled.

'I listened to his messages from that night, just before you came to collect me. I listened.'

'What did he say? Jesus – you should have ...'

'Deleted them? Him?'

He comes towards me, puts an arm around my shoulder. I shake it off.

'You told him about us. Why?'

'Saoirse, look. He was my friend and I just wanted to ... clear the air – have no secrets from my pal ...'

'You wanted to dump your guilt. That's what you wanted.'

'No. I wanted to be straight with him.'

'Sure.'

'Honestly, Saoirse.'

'And then you asked his permission.'

'It wasn't like that.'

'Yes. It was. Like pass the parcel.'

'You're way off ...'

'Finn told me when ye were kids ye were always competing. Toys. Games. Football. That's what it was for you, wasn't it?'

He pushes his hair out of his face, armband like a visible insult. A gaudy joke.

'I thought it was funny at the time – two little boys besting each other.'

'Saoirse, stop. That's not how it was. You know me.'

'Do I?'

'Imagine the guilt I had when ... when he died?'

'Fuck off, Dylan.'

I run. I can feel grass under my bare feet and air whipping my head. I lift my dress so that I can run faster. I head towards the waterfall, careful so that nobody sees me. I throw myself on the grass verge, watching the black, racing water. I could do it. I could sink into cool water, let it envelop me, take me somewhere else. Let it wash the world away. My phone buzzes in my bag. *Fuck off. Everyone. Everything. Just fuck off.*

I close my eyes. Open them again. Stars wink from a navy sky, so many of them. This is how small I am. This is how nothing I am. I stand up, walk towards the water and dip a foot in. The power and force of the flow almost knocks me down. I plant both feet in the cold rush of it and grip the rough pebbled floor with my soles to give anchor. Why? Why can't I let go? The moon is playing tag with the clouds and dances fairy lights across the water. Like a path. I follow the trail of light and there's Finn, across the bank, and Mam's beside him. I can see all his features now, he's not lurking any more and he's with her and I envy them, both of them. She's laughing at something he said and I can hear it crossing the river and filling my ears and stopping the voice notes and their eternal circles.

'Mam, Finn, it's me,' I say into the black night. They both turn together towards me, like they'd choreographed it earlier. Mam stretches her hand up and beckons me and I can nearly smell her from here.

I close my eyes and sink into the water, feel its icy pull. I let it fill me. My ears, eyes, nose. My breath fights against it and my feet scramble for ground. I feel a huge pull and I think now that this is it. *Things I know. Nothing.* Nothing is good. The pull tightens around my waist and guides me to the bank. I fight it but it's no use. Too strong.

I fight harder. Push with my legs and flail with my arms and I'm almost sinking, giving in to the mad silky turmoil, when I spot a tree hanging low over the river, just a few metres away. The water thumps around me, trying to force me away or down. I fight back in angry bursts but I'm so tired and I want to slip into it, let it carry me, enfold me, hug me. I turn my head to check the other bank and they're still there, just watching. If I stop I might drift over towards them. If I stop I might ...

A branch slaps me in the face and I grab it but lose it straight away. I go again, forcing myself up to stretch towards it. This time I hold on, gripping the branch tight as it sways and dips with my weight. My eyes close and the water is velvet and I want to sleep. The branch is strong and I think I could pull myself in to the shore but instead I watch it swaying above my head. I just watch.

'Finn,' I say, but it comes out as a whisper. My face is wet. Tears. Months of tears. I hear their voices calling me. There's nobody on the other bank. I feel myself drifting and shake my head to stay focused. The branch creaks and bends and dances and the water is a powerful rush around me. I could let go. Just let go ...

My hands hurt and I can't remember why I'm here. I can't remember anything. I'm in a river with stars and a donkey crying somewhere and fast cold water and this branch cutting into the flesh on my arms and hands and I have no idea where this is. *Where am I?*

27

I'm still here. Holding on. Finn's beside me, gold football jersey, long, salt-wet hair, a smile that'd floor you.

'How long more?' I say, my words sucked into the swell of the river. 'I can't hold on much longer. It's been hours, maybe days?'

He laughs. Sinks an arm around my waist to take the weight from my hands.

'Are you real?' I shout the words but they're swallowed again into the black void of water.

He smiles and I lean against him and I can feel the weight of him, I'm sure I can, and now I'm laughing and almost lose my grip on the branch but Finn's behind me, holding me tight. It's Finn and I want to ask him why I'm here and where am I going and why he's here too but I can't make the words come out and I can remember his name but not mine and that's the hardest question. *Who am I?*

'She's here, she's over here – in the river,' a voice shouts.

I look back at Finn, but he's gone.

I hear them approach, I hear them running, feet pounding, breath heaving. I don't move, don't open my eyes. I feel a pull around my waist, stronger than water, and I'm lifted through the air. The stars are amazing, confetti in the sky. I'm thrown on the grass and there are figures above me. I splutter and laugh.

'Saoirse?'

I cough up slimy vodka-flavoured water. I'm shivering, my dress clinging to me like wet skin.

'Is she ... is she OK?'

I feel cold hands on my neck.

'She's alive. Thank fuck, she's alive. She must have been in there for a while. Give me something to cover her with – she's frozen. Hey, Saoirse, can you hear me? It's Dad.'

He's trying to lift me and hug me at the same time. I push him away and sit myself up, using the tree as support. I'm blinded by their flashlights and struggle to make out faces. There's a young guy in a suit, cracking his knuckles. Beside him is a girl with deep red hair. Weird looking. My body feels stiff and sore and the man kneeling in front of me is way too close.

'Get away from me,' I say. 'Just fuck off away from me.'

He rises to his feet. 'It's OK, Saoirse, it's fine. We'll get you home and warm and –'

'Who are you?'

'Saoirse ...'

The young guy starts the knuckle-cracking again.

'That'll give you arthritis,' I say.

'I'm sorry, Saoirse.'

'I don't know you.'

'I'm sorry. I just wanted to explain –'

'Stop, Dylan, not now,' says Red Hair.

Who the fuck are these people? The man closest to me, the dad person, takes off his jacket and lays it over me. It has a smell that makes me cry all over again. I'm burying my head in it and wiping my wet face with the sleeve.

'She needs a doctor, Mr Considine,' Knuckle-Cracker says.

'She's my daughter, I'll decide what she needs,' says the dad guy. 'You've caused enough trouble.'

'I didn't do anything. I swear, I didn't.'

'He had the sense to ring you – he did the right thing,' says Red Hair.

'After an hour? Seriously? Why did you wait so long, Dylan? Are you stupid?'

I wipe my face again with the jacket. Tears and snot stain it now and I hold it to my nose, inhaling the smell of it.

'Finn's ... Finn's gone,' I say. I laugh. There's a raw lump in my throat and my head hurts. The dad guy kneels again, reaches out for my hands. I push them behind my back.

'Saoirse. Let's go home.'

'Why are you calling me by that stupid name? Saoirse. Who the fuck is Saoirse?'

'Come on, we'll get you all warm at home. Nana'll be worried. I didn't tell her anything – just ran when I got the call from Dylan, so ...'

'A trip of goats. A drift of hogs. A cast of hawks. A parliament of owls ... who is Saoirse? Just answer me.'

Knuckle-Cracker kneels next to the dad guy.

'Get away from her, you did –'

'Shh, Mr Considine,' he says.

He looks me in the eyes. If he wasn't acting bonkers, he might be handsome.

'Who are you?' he says. 'What's your name?'

I look at the faces in front of me. The light from the torches makes them seem like ghosts. *Who am I?*

'I don't know,' I say.

Things I know. Nothing.

The
In-Between

28

They woke me last night to give me a sleeping tablet. That says it all. They came into my room and shook me until I woke and handed me a pill and a plastic cup of water and told me that this would help me sleep. I took it. I swallowed it. Take the medication. Play the game. That's how you get out. The patient in the bed beside me told me this. She's gone now.

I don't know what day it is but I do know that it's important to know this. This is one of The Questions. There are many. *What's your name? Date of birth? Where do you live? Who do you live with? How do you feel? Tell me about yourself. Can you remember? Who's Finn? Where is he?* I'm learning the answers. Not the real answers – the ones they want to hear. The correct ones. *Saoirse Considine. First of March 2003. Father, sister, brother. Sunflower Cottage, Freagh, Cloughmore. Finn is ... Finn was ... he's in the water.* I need to work on these last questions. They are important because they keep returning to them.

Finn's here. I can feel him. If I wake up from the blue-pill sleep early enough, I can even see him. He comes at dawn, just when the sky is lightening, sometimes streaked and daubed with stripes of pink and purple, sometimes many shades of grey. Always in the same spot, standing near a tree, looking up at my window. I wave sometimes but he's frozen to the tree, like a graffiti person. I don't tell them about Finn.

The nana came today. I nodded. I smiled. I thanked her for the gifts. Chocolate. A book on the brain – who'd even read a book like that? A vegetarian sandwich from a place called The Bad Seed, which, apparently, I love. I hadn't realised I'm meant to be vegetarian. The burgers here are the best thing about the place. And Magda.

It's the father's turn now. The dad. This is how I keep track of time. 'Did you sleep well? Are you getting a good rest? That's all you need, Saoirse, a good rest. Sure the stress and the strain you've been under, what with all that business and Mam and the exams and poor Finn. It's only your brain taking a little break, that's all.'

I smile, nod. I know the routine. I'm afraid to speak in case I mess up. Give the wrong answer.

I didn't sleep last night, or maybe it was the night before, because somebody in another room cried all night and it was the saddest sound. Like a song of sad. The dad can talk. He fills the room with words, words that climb into sentences, paragraphs, whole chapters of a life I'm supposed to know. A jigsaw life of goats and chickens and basil. The whole room is full of his words. I see them on the walls, the ceiling. Like paintings.

*   *   *

Magda's back. It was her day off. She sits with me and there are no questions. Just her. I don't have to turn myself into anyone. Not even Saoirse. Can you have a sense of yourself and not know your name?

I tell her this. 'I know who I am, Magda. I just can't fit it together. It's jumbled up in my head. I don't know what's real and what isn't. I don't know what to tell them and what to leave out. I want to get out of here. If I get out of here, then it will all be fine. I know the smell of the dad person. I know that's real. But I don't know him? It makes my head hurt ...'

She takes off her cleaning gloves, places them on the locker and holds my hand. 'You doing so good, lady. You told me about teacher Sheila on Saturday and how she loved Mr Blake. Poet man. I Google Mr Blake. He is real. You're doing so good, lady.'

Tuesday. Magda told me she would be back on Tuesday. Her son, Jakub, is starting college in Limerick next month. Aeronautical engineering. She's proud of him. Raised him in a strange country all by herself. Her husband beat her and she left him. This is a secret. Something she only tells friends. Magda is an anchor in all the words. She has no history of me. I don't have to be careful.

'Magda, are you real?'

She pinches my hand. It hurts.

'You feel that? Yes? I am real.'

Somebody's singing. It drifts under the door and wakes me from my blue-tablet sleep. Words I know. Melody like the dad smell. It wraps around me, hugs me, goes deep in my head, like it's looking for something. Excavating.

Today is Thursday. Magda reminded me earlier. She cleaned the bathroom and then sat with me. Told me stories about where she grew up. Sopot, part of Tri-City. And the Crooked House. There's a beach too.

'I love beaches, Magda. I swim in the sea all the time ... with my ... with the dad person.'

She beams at this. Magda smiles with her eyes and her mouth and her cheekbones. Can you smile with your cheekbones? She does.

'Baltic Sea not warm. Like Atlantic but colder. You eat today?'

Magda's favourite question.

'Burger, salad, baked potato. Jelly and ice cream.'

'You good lady. I read Mr Blake online. He mad as baskets of frogs.'

I belly laugh. *Like us all, Magda. Like us all.*

*   *   *

I hate this. The nut-job doctor. He stares and taps a pen silently against his wrist like he's timing my answers. Five taps for a correct answer, ten for a wrong one. He stares right inside me, sees thoughts in my head before they've found language. Words. I want to show him how good I am now at the questions but he wants to talk about films I like, books I've read. Songs I sing. I don't know the answers to any of these questions. I have to give him something so I talk about William Blake. How I love him, and teacher Sheila, how I loved her. Five taps. He likes words, the doctor, but only mine. He wants me to cram the room with them, fill the spaces between the taps with strings of them. I talk about the sea. How it controls the moon. Or the moon controls it. I talk about waves and how I saw a body being taken from the sea, limp and floppy and dead. The lungs full of salt water, the hair like ringlets of seaweed, falling down his back. His golden jersey and his swimmer's body, muscled and strong. I tell him that the sea takes at the slightest mistake. When you live by the sea you know this. The sea has no friends. Five taps.

*   *   *

The Knuckle-Cracker's turn. He sits on the chair, all awkward angles. Magda put my hair in plaits. I like them. He stares at them.

'You look ... different ... beautiful ... I mean really nice.'

He shuffles, scrapes the chair on the floor. Makes it squeak. I don't fill in the words for him. He came. He can fill them in himself.

'They told me to talk to you about us ... about you and me. That it'll ... am ... help, like. They said to talk, not to ask you anything. So ... so ... yeah.'

He picks at his nails, then cracks his knuckles. I wince.

'Sorry, it's a nervous habit. Sorry ...'

Sorry. He likes that word.

'I ... am ... can't talk about us unless I start with him.'

I haven't a clue what he's talking about but it's entertaining. Not as good as Magda's stories but amusing all the same.

'I'm no saint ... you know that I shouldn't have said anything to Finn ... I don't know ... It's my fault, it is. I miss him so much ... I'm ... I'm a dumb-ass but you know that ... fuck ...'

He has a sweaty lip and he's talking to his feet.

'I'm not making sense, right? I shouldn't be talking about this ... they told me to but it doesn't feel right. Feels weird, like I'm upsetting you for no fucking good reason ... no rewind, right? That's what you said. But there is. There has to be. It won't be the same but, like ... it will be good. Things get good as well as shit.'

He looks around the room like he's seeking help. His words worm themselves into me. Rewind. Names. Places. Fragments. He's right. None of it makes sense. It could be Magda, talking about her friends. Her other world.

'It'll come back, you know. That's what they're saying.'

I smile because he looks like he's in agony. He breathes out, a deep raggy breath and his shoulders relax.

'Brought you something.'

He bends down and roots in his backpack. He pulls out a silver box. Opens it.

'Want to play?'

I nod. He pulls the locker over and places it between us. I love poker.

29

I wait at the window, watching the sky break into colour. He's there, by his tree, but he won't look up at my window. His hands are stuffed into the pockets of his black jeans. Head down, admiring his feet. Another man approaches with two barky dogs. Finn fades into the tree trunk like a chameleon. I imagine I see his shape in the ridged bark. The shape of Finn.

* * *

The nana brings a boy today and Magda comes in with Polish biscuits and a can of Coke for him.

'You can talk to her, Aran. It's OK.'

The nana pats his shoulder. He plays with a biscuit, turning it over and over in his hand.

'You promised me.' His voice is teenage sing-song. 'You promised and now you're ...'

'Aran, she'll be home soon. Won't you, Saoirse? Your plaits are lovely. I had plaits back in the day. Eva ... Eva's coming soon ... she's upset and she doesn't want you to be upset too. You know what she's like. High drama. Dad dropped us off but they only allow two visitors so he's gone to Aldi.'

The nana loves words. She needs to cram the room with them. She shoos and shepherds them in until there's no space for anything else.

I watch the boy watching his feet. I try to think of something to say that'll make him smile.

'I had to give up the yoga, Saoirse. It gave me awful wind. Did I tell you that when you were in Limerick? And Agnes Flynn died – remember Agnes from two doors down with the drawn-on eyebrows? A stroke she had and all that walking she did out the bank every morning. 'Twas no good to her in the end – she'd have been better off with a few gins and *A Place in the Sun*.'

The boy nibbles a corner of biscuit and sneaks a look at me. I smile, a Magda smile, and he grins back.

'You'll be flying it in a week or two, that's what the doctor says, the long fellow with the weird smell. There's a fancy name and all for what you have – I always feel better when I know the name of things. What's it called now ... am ... associative fugue? No, that's wrong ... *dissociative* fugue. That's it. They love the big words, don't they? I blame the vegetarinarian stuff for your troubles. We're Irish, we need our meat.'

The boy is laughing, silent so the nana doesn't know. I want to laugh, I want to crack up laughing, but I keep my face straight and serious and interested. The nana is talking right at me.

'I'm going back home in time for *A Place in the Sun*. Your father wanted me to come down and stay for a few days, what with the good weather and all, but there's something about that place ... gives me the jitters. They're always watching, waiting for you to put a foot wrong. And they never smile or have an old chat. Aran, you can come home with me – I've a stew on.'

'I'm grand, Nana. I'm going swimming with Dad later.'

He smiles at me. He seems like a nice lad.

Red Hair comes with huge eyes, black with eyeliner, and another gift. Why all the presents?

'Bitch – you're pretending, right? Getting waited on by everyone. I got my horse course. You got your brain course as well – I gave your dad the CAO password. My mam's delighted – so am I – can't wait to get my hands on SUSIE – you know, the student grants? You'll get a great whack off SUSIE cos you're living in the sticks, like – is there anything to eat?'

She's the queen of words. I like her.

*   *   *

It's Tuesday again. Magda had her hair done at the weekend. Shorter but it suits her. She's wearing glittery eye-shadow and gold stud earrings. She's angry today. I haven't seen Angry Magda before.

'He – landlord – say I go – he selling house. Lies. I told him you are liar. I must find house now. He is – what you say? Prick. He is prick.'

'Excellent choice, Magda. Prick.'

'He big prick.'

'Huge prick.'

She starts to laugh and then we're both cracking up, her cleaning trolley forgotten.

'You good person, Saoirse. You like jokes. Good people like jokes.'

It's raining, so the sunrise is just a paling of the sky. Rain smatters the window and I can hear the constant drone of it on the roof. No Finn. I keep my eyes on the tree because I know how he can paint himself into the bark of it. He's not there. Gone. I feel relief. He was just something to watch. That's all.

*　　*　　*

A new person comes to share the room with me. She's tiny. I can see her bones through her T-shirt; her arms are thin as fingers.

'I want to go home. I hate it here. I want to go home.'

I watch her from my bed. Her head is bent into her chest. She's hugging her knees and rocking back and forth. And crying. Painful and bleating. I walk over and sit on the bed beside her, afraid to touch her. There are crisscross marks on her wrists, angry red welts of pain.

'You can't be sad. They lock you up for being sad. I want to go home. I want my mam.'

She looks at me, her eyes huge in her bony face. I pull her towards me. Allow her to cry. She is so small in my arms. I can feel the broken in her.

*　　*　　*

She comes in a blur of blond hair and clattering heels and a belly top. The top is the colour of sun. She fills the room, not with words, but with light, like she's shining.

'You're having a grand handy summer. Dad made me clean out the chicken shed yesterday. Fuck sake, like, Saoirse – look. Broke my nail and all and they're just done fresh. Look – fucking ruined it is. And the smell? Christ – you'll never catch me eating oats and seeds and shit if that's what it produces. Rotten.'

She plonks a make-up box up on the bed.

'Come on – nails first. You look like a madwoman.'

We laugh and I give her my hand. She shakes her head.

'A mess. You were biting them. I'll have to file the shit out of them now.'

She takes out a file and starts to work. Her touch is light and knowing.

'She asleep?'

I nod.

'I can do hers too if she wakes up. Why's your hair like your wan out of *The Little House on the Prairie*? I'll be here all day, fixing you.'

Things I know. Eva.

December

30

I can see the river from the balcony. I have to lean out a little, but I can see the grey expanse winding through trees. Up here, you feel like you're in the trees. I'm sharing with three others. Chinese, Irish, American. We're like the United Nations. All colours and creeds. The kitchen smells like the spice stalls in the Milk Market.

What to wear? Eva sent me instructions earlier. Photos of suitable winter attire. Her #OOTD. Inappropriate short skirt with a plunging-neckline top and six-inch stilettos. The old Saoirse would be horrified. This Saoirse realises that her sister is way funnier than her. I'm tempted to dress like that and send her a Snapchat.

What to wear? I sit on the edge of the narrow bed. I'm in my raggy Simpsons T-shirt and my knickers. The top has holes in it, a remnant from my childhood. I want to wear this: it straddles both worlds; it knows all my history. I push two fingers through a gash below the neckline. I think it's on its last legs – for bed only. What to wear, so? I pull on a pair of black jeans and a grey T-shirt. Mark Zuckerberg style. Anonymous, chameleon. I plait my hair in Magda fashion and slip on my Cons.

I take the long way around so that I can enjoy the full expanse of the river. This place is a Utopia, a self-sufficient island. A fortress protected from outside threats. It has just rained and I get the river smell, mixed with winter decay and earth. The sun struggles to overcome dark, rolling clouds. The clouds win and threaten to spill their guts on this island with its fancy bridges and buildings. I reach the square. Right in the middle there's a statue of a man – Brown Thomas they call him – and he always makes me sad. I enter the main building with its ski-slope glass front. It's a maze. There is no logic to the floor plan. The architect was drunk or just having a laugh. I wander into various rooms before I find the right one. I sit in the waiting room. No candles. No mental health slogans. That's a good start. I feel calm but I know it's the medication working. Even-keel tablets. My phone beeps. A snap from Aran of Izzy Goat at the kitchen window.

A tall, angular woman calls me into her office. I sit opposite her, surveying the room. View of the river from the window. No salt lamps. Books on psychology on the bookshelf. A handmade card on the windowsill. *The coolest mom in the world.* Running shoes in the corner. A set of small weights. She's reading notes. Her glasses suit her.

'Saoirse, I'm Sadhbh,' she says, offering her hand. 'You got stuck with a weird Irish name too? I win with the consonants – a right mouthful. Did you have trouble finding the place? That was a stupid question – of course you did.'

I laugh. I like her. There's a picture on her desk of the happy family. Two mams and two daughters. She sees me looking at it.

'Don't worry. We gave them sensible names – Jen and Amy.'

'Perfect,' I say. 'They'll be grand in Starbucks.'

She laughs this time. 'We are liaising with your care team, Saoirse – you know that already. I have all your notes and reports. I'd like to hear from you. All I know for now is that you have a weird name like me.'

She leans back and lets the words sit between us. So do I. She's good, though, just sits there, at ease with herself.

I won't talk, I won't say anything. I can't spread myself around any more. I'm running out of me. There's not enough to go around.

Her face is neutral, her body still. I fix my eyes on a picture on the wall. It's her, winning some kind of race. Her wife's hugging her at the finish line.

'I miss Finn.'

She nods.

I pick my thumbnail. 'Everybody. The doctors. Nana and Dad. Dylan. All of them, they didn't know him, not really. I miss him so much and ... I blame myself still.'

A slight incline of her head. No words. She has taken out a sheet of paper and is drawing something on it. It feels like permission to say whatever I want.

'First Mam and then Finn and it's ... it was like everything I touched died and ...'

She looks up, holds my gaze. Nods. The nods are like traffic lights. Permission.

'I forgot things and didn't ... I didn't know. And time was all ... bent and weird and I ... I was sad.'

She's back to drawing.

'I miss Finn.'

She smiles and pushes the paper towards me. It's a graph – a stress graph.

'You're up here,' she says, pointing to the highest line. 'This one down here is what would be considered "normal". We have to figure out how your level climbed so high. I believe you.'

Silence settles in again. She wears it like a comfortable throw.

'I felt angry and sad when we moved ... after Mam ... It was like Dad wanted to erase her, you know, not walk the same streets and go to the same places and see her every-where. But I still saw her. I saw her all the time and then Finn and ... and it was up to me to fix things and I didn't ... I couldn't.'

'Angry?'

'Angry. I got angry with Finn too. With his black moods, his gambling. You know when you start going out with someone? It's all shiny and lovely and then ... the dark stuff ... moods ... compulsions ... I'm not naïve – I know that things change, but when you're feeling low yourself and this happens and ... I had to end it with him ... I had to ...'

I feel tears coming. Malcolm would be delighted with a few tears. She remains silent. Impassive.

'It all got too big. All of it. I ended it. The others walked away from me – like they were just waiting for the chance. There was Dylan, but even that turned out to be a bit shit ... sorry.'

'You're fine, Saoirse.'

'I bit Cian Burke – is that in the notes? It should be because Dr Death in Ennis was obsessed with that.'

She nods and I imagine I see a tiny smile.

'The hate in the town after that, when I walked down the street. You could nearly touch the hate. And everybody at home was sad and I couldn't fix it, couldn't undo the stuff or change it.'

There's a rock in my throat and I have to cry to ease the pain. A good cry, a shoulder-shake one with snot. She hands me a bunch of tissues. I realise I'm wailing and try to quieten myself so that I don't put off the next client. She sits there, calm and silent. It feels like ages before the tears lessen and the shake is a shudder.

'I'm sorry.'

'No need to be sorry. This is what I'm here for.'

I gulp in air and scrub at my eyes. The tissue is sodden already.

'I started to feel outside of myself. Does that make sense? I fought with Jade – she had a crap boyfriend – and I missed her too and ...'

The tears are back and the rock has re-formed in my throat and I can't get words out. She lets me cry and blow rivers of snot into a fresh bunch of tissues. This woman, this epitome of stillness, can get me to spill my guts without saying one word. I feel tired and shaky.

'How can I know what's real and what isn't? Are my opinions of things just my paranoia? Am I imagining the whole town hates me? Can I trust myself?'

'It's good to question everything. There are truths in there. It'll take time, but we'll sieve through the lot.'

I look up from a wad of tissue. 'Really?'

'Yes. Of course. What's the thing you couldn't say?'

I shake my head.

'It's fine. We'll get to all of it eventually.'

'I find it hard to ... to like myself.'

I fist away tears and my eyes feel raw. I watch her face as she looks at me. It's open – there are no questions here, no right answers, no slogans and shopping lists.

'Allow yourself to feel everything.'

I reach in for another bunch of tissues. The box is almost empty. 'What if ... what if it happens again? What if I just go off on one of my loopy trips and forget who I am?'

She shakes her head. 'I think that's enough for today. I want you to think about one thing.'

'OK?' My voice is stringy with snot and tears.

'Who owns what?' she asks.

'I don't understand.'

'It's your dad's grief. Those friends in Cloughmore – it's their behaviour. You don't own any of that. You can only control what you own yourself.'

She's gathering her notes and I'm stuck to the chair

with her simple words. What do I own in all of it? What do I control? What can I control?

'Am ... can I ask you something?'

'Sure.'

'Medication. I hate it. And I hate the day hospital in town – all they do is hand out pills and that's not good either, is it? They've got a pill for everything.'

'Is it helping at the moment?'

I think about this. The anxiety is improving; my volcano stomach is dormant. The day hospital causes anxiety – two-hour waits and you never see the same doctor – but the medication seems to work.

'I think so. Yes.'

'There you go. Let's work our way through everything over the next while, medication included. I'll explain how it works in our next session, possible side effects, how we can work towards your being medication-free down the road. One step at a time. It's not a race.'

'Thank you,' I say. 'Thank you so much.'

'You're welcome. I'll see you weekly from now on and we can continue. Same time next week?'

I nod. 'Will it be you I see again?'

'Of course. We'll get through this – we'll sort it out. It's fine.'

She smiles and I believe her. I wish I could see her again tomorrow. I wish I could bring her home with me.

*   *   *

The sun has won the cloud fight. The square is college-busy now. There's a small quartet set up by the green area and their sound drifts over the knots of people milling around. There's also a food truck and the pungent smell of chips makes me think of holidays. And of Lord's Cove and salt-thick air.

He's sitting on one of the long benches, legs outstretched, face turned up towards the sun. I watch him for a minute, admire the jib of him.

I'm leaning on Brown Thomas, pressing my head into his cool chest. I root in my backpack for water and slug back a huge gulp. I walk over to him.

He seems to be asleep. I bend and shout into his ear.

'Dylan. Get up for school.'

He jumps, and students nearby laugh.

'Jesus, you absolute gowl.'

'How're things? Where are the others?'

He smiles. There are splashes of paint in his hair. He looks different, like the rural edges of him have been smoothed out. Like he's found his place.

'I had to stay up all night to finish a project – and it's crap, Saoirse. I thought I could draw until I started in art college. I'm useless.'

'That's why you're in college, you gowl.'

I sit down beside him, lean against his shoulder.

'Where's your car?' I say. 'Did you have to pay for parking?'

'Are you joking? I'm way too smart for that. Here they come.'

Jade and Luke stroll towards us, both talking with mad hand gestures. My heart thumps and blood fills my ears. Luke sees us, sees me, and he's loping over, backpack slung across his shoulder. He leans down, kisses me.

'Get a fucking room, lads,' says Jade. 'Seriously – ye're disgusting. Aren't they, Dylan?'

Dylan laughs. 'Luke – you'd better behave on your first trip to Cloughmore. Saoirse's dad's a tank.'

'Am I making a big mistake? Bringing this fella home to eggs and goats and you crazies?'

Dylan laughs. 'At last.'

I look at him. 'What do you mean?'

He shrugs. 'Home. Cloughmore. You're one of us now.'

Luke pulls me up with his hand.

'Does anybody want to know about a horse's digestive system because it's truly rank – I swear,' says Jade. 'Which way is the car, Dylan? Luke, are we stupid to be going to Cloughmore for a weekend – like, seriously? What'll we do?'

'We've horses on our farm,' says Dylan.

'I don't want to see a fucking horse for a month. A year even,' she says.

'Can we get chips first?' says Luke. 'I'm starving – no breakfast and back-to-back lectures.'

'Luke never misses a lecture – nerdy Luke,' I say.

He bends down and kisses me again. I grab his face and kiss him back.

'For fuck sake,' says Jade.

'Chips,' I say. 'Big fat greasy ones from Luigi's.'

'No way,' says Jade. 'Chicken Hut. The best place in town. Anywhere else feels like cheating.'

Luke slides his hand into mine and we walk in the path of the December sun. Dylan and Jade are trailing us, laughing at something.

Things I know. This.

ACKNOWLEDGEMENTS

I'd like to thank all of the people who spoke to me while researching this book. That includes the professionals, the patients and sufferers, the mental health advocates. Thank you so much for your candour and honesty.

Thank you to my friends and family for support while working on this book. (The family support is negligible!) Thanks to Jimi Kavanagh for tech queries. A special thank you to Rena Roohipour and Mary Coll, who are always my first readers and thus subjected to many iterations of the story. Thanks to Limerick Arts Office, who are so supportive of my work, and to the Tyrone Guthrie Centre for the peace to write and the fabulous food.

Thank you to Archie Cat and his servants, Niamh, Evie and Esme, for allowing me to use his adventures.

Thank you to my best girls, my dogs, Bonnie and Kali, for the foot-warming company and Chicken Hut for the garlic cheese chips on demand (fork's in the bag, you gowl). Thanks also to Strange Boy (@StrangeBoyWha) for his brilliant *Holy/Unholy*, which became the soundtrack to my huge rewrite.

A final thank you to my MVP, my editor and publisher Siobhán Parkinson. Her advice was invaluable and she brought out the real story in her gentle, intelligent way. I loved working with her on this book. *Go raibh míle maith agat*.

The Gone Book

I know you'll hate me.
I just know you will.
But I can't help it.
I'm going to find you.

Matt's mam left home when he was 10. He writes letters to her but doesn't send them. He keeps them in his Gone Book, which he hides in his room. Five years of letters about his life. Five years of hurt.

Matt's dad won't talk about her. His older brother is mixed up with drugs and messing with dangerous characters. His friends, Mikey and Anna, are the best thing in his life, but Matt keeps pushing them away.

All Matt wants to do is skate, surf, and forget. But now his mam is back in town and Matt knows he needs to find her, to finally deliver the truth.

About Helena Close

From Limerick City in the west of Ireland, Helena Close has been writing full-time for twenty years. She has written or co-written seven novels, published by Hodder Headline (under the pseudonym Sarah O'Brien), Hachette Ireland and Blackstaff Press. *Things I Know* is her second young adult novel.

'Extraordinary, a remarkable book that expands the frontiers of Irish popular fiction.'

The Irish Times (for *The Cut of Love*)

'An impressive, relevant, and entertaining read. An absolute page turner.'

The Irish Independent (for *The Clever One*)

About Little Island

Little Island publishes the best new Irish writing for young readers. Founded in 2010 by Ireland's first Laureate na nÓg (children's laureate), Siobhán Parkinson, Little Island remains Ireland's only independent English-language press specialising in books for children and teens.

RECENT AWARDS
FOR LITTLE ISLAND BOOKS

Book of the Year, KPMG Children's Books Ireland Awards 2021
Savage Her Reply by Deirdre Sullivan

YA Book of the Year, Literacy Association of Ireland Awards 2021
Savage Her Reply by Deirdre Sullivan

YA Book of the Year, An Post Irish Book Awards 2020
Savage Her Reply by Deirdre Sullivan

White Raven Award 2021
The Gone Book by Helena Close

Judges' Special Prize, KPMG Children's Books Ireland Awards 2020
The Deepest Breath by Meg Grehan

Shortlisted: The Waterstones Children's Book Prize 2020
The Deepest Breath by Meg Grehan

Little Island

Books create waves